What the experts are saying about

Leonardo da Vinci Gets A Do-Over

Innovators in Action!

Leonardo da Vinci
Gets A Do-Over

Mark P. Friedlander, Jr.

Science, Naturally!®
Washington, DC

First print edition • November 2014
E-book edition   • November 2014

Paperback ISBN 13: 978-0-9678020-6-0 • ISBN 10: 0-9678020-6-7
E-book   ISBN 13: 978-0-9700106-4-3 • ISBN 10: 0-9700106-4-8

Published in the United States by:
  Science, Naturally! LLC
  725 8th Street, SE • Washington, DC 20003
  202-465-4798 • Toll-free: 1-866-SCI-9876 (1-866-724-9876)
  Fax: 202-558-2132
  Info@ScienceNaturally.com • www.ScienceNaturally.com

Distributed to the book trade by:
  National Book Network
  Toll-free: 800-462-6420 • Fax: 800-338-4550
  CustomerCare@nbnbooks.com • www.nbnbooks.com

Teacher's Guide available at www.ScienceNaturally.com

Library of Congress Cataloging-in-Publication Data
  Friedlander, Mark P., author.
  Leonardo da Vinci gets a do-over / Mark P. Friedlander, Jr. -- First print edition.
    pages cm. -- (Innovators in action! ; 1)
  Summary: "The passing of great Renaissance master Leonardo da Vinci- artist, anatomist,
  engineer, inventor- marked the end of an era. The world hasn't seen a visionary like him
  since...until now. On a school trip to Florence, three American middle school students think
  they're in for a treat when a man who claims to be Leonardo da Vinci, brought back to life
  with a mission to better humankind, crashes their tour. Too bad he isn't really the celebrated
  Master of the Renaissance...or is he? Will the students be able to help Leonardo evade the
  mayor of Florence's selfish grasp so he can complete his quest before his time runs out? Tag
  along with Tad, Max, and Gina as they assist Leonardo on his quest, discover the secrets of
  his life, and teach the Maestro about science, math, history, art, and more!"-- Provided by
  publisher.
  Audience: Ages 10-14.
  Audience: Grades 7 to 8.
  Includes bibliographical references and index.
  ISBN 978-0-9678020-6-0 (pbk.) -- ISBN 978-0-9700106-4-3 (ebook)
  1. Leonardo, da Vinci, 1452-1519--Juvenile literature. 2. Inventors--Italy--Biography--
Juvenile literature. 3. Artists--Italy--Biography--Juvenile literature. 4. Florence (Italy)--21st
century--Juvenile fiction. I. Title.
  T40.L46F75 2014
  709.2--dc23

10 9 8 7 6 5 4 3 2 1

Schools, libraries, government, and non-profit organizations can receive a bulk
discount for quantity orders. Please contact us at the address above or email us at
Info@ScienceNaturally.com

Printed in the United States of America

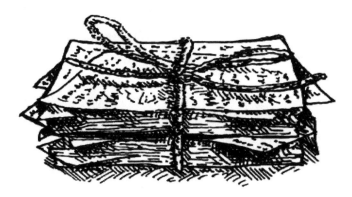

This book is dedicated…

… to my wife, Dorothy, who was with me in Florence when she and I first discovered the world of Leonardo da Vinci in May 2000,

and

… to the gang: A.J., Kevin, Amy, Ariel, Erin, Blake, Christopher, Drew, Lucas, Matthew, Cort, Will, David, Moshe, Jamie and Kyle.

Supporting and Articulating Curriculum Standards

Science, Naturally books
address two dimensions of the
Next Generation Science Standards:
Disciplinary Core Ideas and
Cross-Cutting Concepts.

All Science, Naturally books align with
the Common Core State Standards.

The content also aligns with
the math and science
standards laid out by the
Center for Education at the National Academies.

Articulations to these, and other standards,
are available at
www.ScienceNaturally.com.

Teacher's Guide Available!

Expand and extend the learning experience
with our teacher-written study guide.
Download at www.ScienceNaturally.com

Additional Resources

Take advantage of the glossary, a biography of
Leonardo da Vinci and suggestions for continued
reading at the back of this book.

Welcome to Florence!

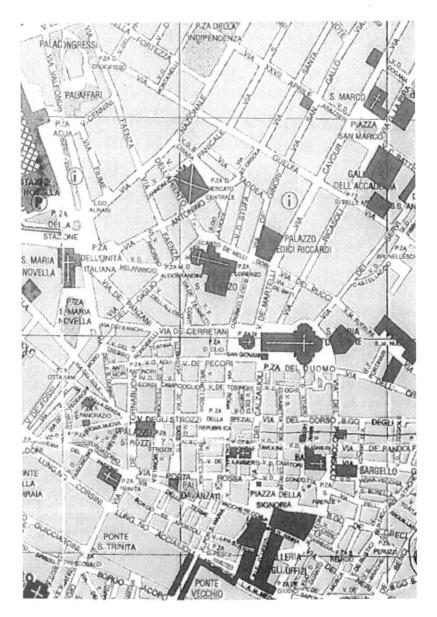

This map was prepared by Lorenzo Gualtieri and printed here
by permission from the Department of Tourism, Florence, Italy.

From learned men I quickly found
Their knowledge was jejune
Ignorance was world around
I've been born too soon.

So this what you need to know
As I hasten to explain.
Just watch for purple mist
Where I shall appear again!

Translated from a Leonardo da Vinci codex
… yet to be discovered.

Table of Contents

Why I Wrote This Book

Mark P. Friedlander, Jr.

Throughout my life, I have been fortunate to travel to many parts of the world. In May 2000, I visited Italy with my wife, Dorothy. When we arrived in the ancient city of Florence, I was enchanted. I felt like I was back in the Renaissance—that period in history when the slumbering world of the Middle Ages awoke to a revival of art and intellectual inquiry.

Surrounded by the ghosts of such brilliant and talented men as da Vinci, Galileo, and Michelangelo, I began to wonder how I would explain our modern world to them if I were their tour guide to the 21st century. There are so many ordinary things that we use or do today that would be a mystery to a time traveler from five centuries ago (just as many of the things they used and did may seem strange to us).

A few years later, I was invited by the founder of *Science, Naturally* to submit a manuscript for a middle school book that blended real science and mathematics into a work of fiction. My mind flashed back to those magical days spent in Florence. It was immediately clear to me that I would invite Leonardo da Vinci to be my ambassador. Through my characters, I could live out my fantasy of playing tour guide to the Maestro himself, all the while learning about Renaissance science, math, and history from him.

To tackle this project, I had to engage in serious research, earnest book learning, and a lot of imagination—but it soon became a labor of love. So, pull up your favorite chair, grab some *gelato*, and get ready to follow the antics of Leonardo, Gina, Max, and Tad as they explore 21st century Florence. *Arrivederci!*

-Mark

PROLOGUE

Leonardo da Vinci's last memory was of dying. It was May 2, 1519. The room was sealed from the glorious spring weather by massive, tightly drawn curtains. Only a few candles flickered in the room, allowing for the darkness that suited death. Outside of Clos Lucé, the manor house provided to him by the King of France, Francis I, the sun-splashed spring day was filled with the songs of birds and the distant sounds of people. Leonardo was perched on thickly piled pillows. His entourage, including King Francis I, himself, was gathered beside his bed for what were to be Leonardo da Vinci's final hours.

As he lay in bed, he felt life ebbing from him. For months, he suffered from a paralysis of his right arm and part of the right side of his face. For this ailment, he was treated with salves extracted from herbs and local plants, but, as he had suspected, they didn't work.

The last thing that rang in his ears on that final day was the words a strange gypsy woman uttered when she slipped into his bedroom a few days before. His memory of the ragged gypsy's visit was blurry at best—if it had indeed been an actual occurrence and not just the feverish dreams of a dying man.

He opened his eyes at the sound of footsteps, heavy breathing, and a foul odor to see a woman make her way to the edge of his bed. She was bent with age, shaggily dressed, and cloaked in a tattered shawl. He tried to cry out, but could not emit any audible sounds. He could only watch her, suspicious and curious of her intentions as she stopped at the side of his bed.

The old woman shook her head and muttered inaudibly. Then, raising her eyes and her arms toward the ceiling, she spoke loudly in a Vlax Romani dialect Leonardo recognized but did not understand. The curtains began to sway, but there was no breeze. The gypsy seemed to take the mysterious movement as a response to her query as she nodded and turned back to look down at Leonardo once more.

Then she spoke again, softly this time and as if speaking from the bottom of a well. He did not know the language, but strangely, he understood. As she spoke, he drifted in and out of slumber.

"Leonardo da Vinci, son of the high born notary, Ser Piero da Vinci, and Caterina, a peasant woman, with whom he was not joined by law or the divine, your birth into this life was not as planned," crooned the gypsy. "You were destined for the future. Your birth was a mistake. To correct this, you will be given a second chance, an opportunity to do what you might have done. This do-over is yours because your potential has yet to be reached. You have more to give. But know this," she warned, raising a crooked finger, "If you do not wish to die a second and more painful death, you must not waste your genius. You must invent or discover something that benefits all mankind."

Those were the last words Leonardo remembered, but he had dismissed them as a voice in a dream. But now, those words rang in his ears. The doubt he had felt about her pronouncement vanished.

Leonardo had no clear idea how much time had passed between his death and the present moment. All he knew was that he was now twisting slowly in a vortex of swirling mist. To fly had been his biggest dream. During his life, he had tried to design a flying machine. Now he was flying, without a machine.

Leonardo filled thousands of pages with notes and drawings during his lifetime, recording all of his ideas and thoughts. But here in this vortex, as he considered the gypsy's prediction, he could not recall anything he had done that had been remarkable. He had had many ideas, but never put any of them to use. He designed inventions that he never went on to build. He realized that he had rarely finished a project, except for a handful of paintings for which he had been paid a fee. He worked for over four years on his favorite painting, the *Mona Lisa*, but when he died, he still felt that it was a work-in-progress. He wondered now what had become of his cherished painting.

As he rose steadily upward, he understood that his death took place a very long time ago—though he had no idea how much time had passed. He became aware that he was growing younger and younger. Waving his right arm, he was astonished to find it was no longer paralyzed. He shouted into the dense mist for the joy of the moment, his voice clear and strong. Strength returned to his body. A thrill surged through him as he understood that he was, indeed, alive again.

Slowly, the mist turned from white to red. The red deepened as he turned and examined his hands. They were not the wrinkled and gnarled hands he remembered from his deathbed, but instead the slender, powerful hands of middle years.

The mist slowly changed from red to orange, and the orange lightened to yellow, as though Leonardo were being transported through a prism. He waved his right arm again, but it had no effect on the mist. He continued to slowly twist and rise, lifted by an invisible but gentle force.

From yellow, the mist turned to green. He studied his hands again, bending and straightening his fingers nimbly. He lifted his long beard and saw it had become a thick golden yellow. As the mist darkened from green to blue, he began to hear sounds. There were voices in the distance and a strange whirring and humming he could not identify. Darkening more, the mist turned blue, then shifted to a deep, rich purple. The mist hissed loudly, the spinning increased, and a powerful wind whipped his tunic, making him shudder.

Then, as if he had just stepped onto a stage, he felt hard ground beneath his feet.

In that instant, the wind, the spinning, and the howling all stopped. The air was suddenly still, and he found himself standing on a rough, gray street among a crowd of people. Their clothing was strange—many of the women and all of the men were wearing trousers, but no cloaks, and the skirts the women wore were much shorter than were customary for women in his lifetime. Some of the younger men and women wore shirts with strange writing on them. The people stood taller, talked faster, and with a different dialect. Their hair was cut shorter. Some walked about with white smoking sticks in their mouths. The place was familiar, but also strange.

He looked around. No one seemed to notice his arrival. They were all chasing papers and hats blown by the brief burst of wind. The envelope of mist and clouds was gone. His eyes adjusted to the beautiful sunlit day. Amid the distracted crowd of people, he realized he was standing in the middle of the central piazza of Florence, a piazza he knew well. He remembered some of the buildings and marveled at others. The giant statue of David still stood. He was back in the Piazza della Signoria in his beloved Florence. He was home.

1. THE MEETING

Dr. Willard Kastleboro was a dark-haired, slightly balding middle school history teacher whose academic passion was the Renaissance. He was average in height—well, maybe slightly less than average—and still trim enough to wear a belt without the need for suspenders. One part of his job that he particularly enjoyed was leading field trips with some of his eighth grade students.

He favored taking students to famous cities in Italy, perhaps because they were steeped in history-rich culture that could bring more meaning to his lessons. Or maybe it was simply because he spoke fluent Italian. Privately, he admitted that he quite enjoyed showing off his advanced language skills in front of his students.

On this particular trip, he was joined by two colleagues. One was Emily Willoughby, a tall and self-possessed math teacher. The other was Gabrielle Howdershell, a brilliant teacher who was regarded as a walking encyclopedia of science.

Last year, Dr. Kastleboro and a few of his co-workers had taken a group of students to Rome to get a feel for the history of the Roman Empire. The year before, he led a group to Venice to study the 14th century trade wars between Venice and its rival city-state, Genoa. It was now the year 2000, and they were on the cusp of a new and promising century. The group was in Florence to study Leonardo da Vinci in the birthplace of the Renaissance. The teachers planned to offer lessons derived from a study of the 15th and 16th centuries, along with an understanding of the world during the Middle Ages. It was a time when Europeans had begun to search for a better understanding of the world in which they lived.

On an early afternoon, Max, Tad, and Gina accompanied Dr. Kastleboro to visit the famous Piazza della Signoria. The three were finishing their final semester in middle school and were anxiously looking forward to the excitement and challenges of high school. Their close friendship was a mystery to their classmates, since their backgrounds were vastly different. Even so, their new relationship was strong. In fact, it had only been three months since they had first met.

ℰᴈℂℛ

Tad, whose full name was Theodore Jefferson Sullivan, had arrived at Longfellow Middle School in Falls Church, Virginia, just as the new semester began in January. His family's arrival in Northern Virginia was an exciting beginning in his life. The suburban surroundings were in stark contrast to his earlier years in Rivertown.

At 14, he was older than most of his classmates. Growing taller over the past year, he felt awkward at this new height. The ever expanding distance from his eyes to his feet required him to readjust how he walked and ran. His skinny boyish body was transforming into one belonging to a strong and hearty young man.

His family moved to Falls Church when Tad's father was offered a new job. For Tad, the new school was a welcome change. He had not been happy in Rivertown, a small mill town nestled in a valley in the Appalachian Mountains of southwest Virginia. It seemed to Tad that most of his school days at Rivertown Middle School had been devoted to avoiding his predator, Mike Baldwin. The bully tripped Tad in the hallway, stole his homework, snatched his lunch, and called him names like "moron," "lame brain," and—Mike's personal favorite— "Taddy-Waddy."

Tad never told his parents or anyone else how he was treated because that would only reveal his own cowardice, and Rivertown was not a place for sissies or crybabies. Some of his friends told him to stand up and fight, but he was too afraid to try. Luckily, his family moved before things escalated any further. By January, Tad was in a new school and a new community, far away from Mike and Rivertown.

It was cold and blusterous on that first day Tad stepped off of the school bus and followed the stream of students flowing into the crowded halls. This was his chance to reinvent himself. No one at this school knew him yet. Here, he could be confident and cool. All he had to do was act sure of himself and no one would know he felt the opposite. Searching the locker numbers along the hall, he quickly found the one assigned to him.

While he was storing his new books and his jacket, he noticed a tall boy jamming his finger against the chest of a smaller boy. The tall boy had brown hair, angry eyes, pale skin, and a sharp, nasal voice. The smaller boy was dark-skinned, with sparkling brown eyes that shone behind round, black-rimmed glasses. In contrast to the other casually dressed students, he wore a white shirt and a red bow tie. Tad stopped putting away his books and watched.

"You're new here, aren't you?" jeered Neville, the taller boy.

"That's true," answered Max, the shorter boy.

Max's real name was Harlan Maxfield Peabody. From an early age, he was often teased because of his name, so he decided to just go by Max. He wasn't sure why Neville was hostile, but he figured he'd learn soon enough. He straightened his back, standing as tall as his limited height would allow, but he was still a few inches shorter than Neville.

From the time he was two years old, Max showed a remarkable talent for numbers. His parents were astounded when he began lining his numbered blocks up in numerical sequence. By the age of four he could add, subtract, multiply and divide numbers in his head.

As he grew, his Uncle Bill urged him to practice shooting baskets. "Basketball is the sport of kings," his uncle said. When it became apparent that Max was not going to be tall like his brothers, his uncle switched his campaign to golf. "Great game, golf. No size requirement, but you have to learn young. Sports, boy, sports are where you make your fortune." Then he'd chuckle. "Unless you can sing or dance. But you can't."

His mother, on the other hand, would always pull him aside after a visit with Uncle Bill and say, "Listen, Max, my brother means well, but don't listen to him. Study hard. You can do whatever you put your mind to."

Neville shoved Max against the lockers, sneering. "You know, you're pretty short for your size, kid."

"No," replied Max, fixing his glasses. "I'm just short for my age."

"You some kind of wise guy?" Neville gave Max another shove.

At that moment, Tad took a deep breath to summon some courage, reminding himself that he had no history of cowardice here, and stepped into the confrontation. "Hey, whatcha doing picking on a smaller guy?"

"Butt out," replied Neville, looking at Tad, who was as tall as he was, but heftier, and then back at Max.

Tad took a step forward. No one spoke.

Then Neville sneered, "I should have noticed before. You two look alike. You must be brothers." Leaning close to Max, he added, "Listen, short stuff, I know who you are. They call you Mathematical Max. Every year, the school has a math competition. I won last year, and I plan to win this year. I don't know if you're really a math whiz or all talk, but stay out of the contest. Just remember that I'm the president of our class, and if I like you, then your life in this school can be very pleasant. On the other hand, if I don't ..." He stopped, paused, looked at Tad, then back at Max. "Just don't enter."

Max cocked his head, adjusted his glasses again, and spoke. "Thanks for telling me about the contest. I'm sure I'll be entering."

"Best you don't," Neville said, eyes flashing.

"This meeting is over," said Tad, moving slowly toward Neville, who turned and walked toward his next class.

"Just don't, short stuff," Neville called back before he was out of earshot.

Max and Tad watched as he disappeared into the crowd of students.

"Thanks," said Max, holding out his arm to Tad for a fist bump. "I'm Max."

Tad returned the fist bump. "I'm Tad," he said. "What was that about?"

Max answered, "I have no idea, but if it involves math, then I want to be in it."

"Who was that guy?"

"Neville Kraxton. Believe it or not, he's the eighth grade class president."

"Has he been bullying you?"

"This is the first time, but it probably won't be the last," Max said glumly.

"You can count on me to help out," said Tad, gathering his books. "See you in the lunch hall, okay? We newcomers need to stick together."

"Great," replied Max, knocking his glasses crooked as he put on his backpack.

ഇറോ

They met for lunch in the school cafeteria every day after that. Soon, Max and Tad noticed a girl sitting alone. At the table next to her, other girls were laughing and talking; they seemed to be deliberately ignoring her. They looked at each other and, without saying anything, walked over.

She had deep brown eyes and wavy chestnut hair past her shoulders. "Mind if we join you?" asked Tad. "We, uh, need your expertise on something."

The girl's eyes lit up. She smiled, revealing a mouth full of metal.

"I'm Tad. This is my friend, Max."

"Hi." Max smiled as they sat down.

"Max?" She raised her eyebrows in question. "Aren't you the guy they call Mathematical Max?"

"That's me," replied Max.

"I'm very happy to meet you, both of you." She didn't want them to feel sorry for her, but she had been watching them during lunch and had secretly hoped that one of them would talk to her. They seemed friendly. "I know you guys made up an excuse to join me, but it's so great that you did." The girl was known for never being anything less than blunt and direct.

"Well, we—" Tad began.

"And I want you to know I'm honestly grateful," she interrupted. "I'm new this semester, and the other girls haven't welcomed me. They think I'm too fat and my big braces make me look ugly. I've noticed you two at lunchtime and saw that you weren't hanging with the other guys. I haven't made any friends here yet. I've been living with my family in Italy for three years, so everything here is new, and to tell you the truth, I've been really lonely."

"Wow," said Max. "You sure are a fast talker."

"And a straight talker," said Tad. "What's your name?"

"Oh, sorry," she said. "I'm Gina."

Within a short time, Gina became the third member of this unlikely group. Her mother was Italian and had met and married Gina's father during his first tour of duty at the naval base in Naples, her hometown. As the child of an active duty officer in the United States Navy, Gina had lived on naval bases throughout the world.

Dr. Kastleboro and the teachers welcomed her to join them on the Florence trip in the spring, pleased that she spoke fluent Italian. Tad and Max were glad she was going because she was always pleasant and outspoken and made them feel comfortable with whatever subject they discussed.

Later that week, Max, Tad, and Gina gathered at lunch to prepare for the upcoming math competition.

Every year, Ms. Willoughby hosted the school's *Math Madness* competition the week before spring break. The contest this year was to come up with an exciting way to explain the size of a billion and present it in an educational outreach project to a fourth grade class at a nearby elementary school. The prize for the winner, or winning group, was exemption from the mid-semester examination.

She explained to the class that the previous year's winning group, led by Neville Kraxton, came up with a mathematical way to calculate the height of the school flag pole. They did this by using the ratio of the length of the shadow of a yardstick to the length of the shadow of the flag pole. Neville had held up a yardstick and measured the length of its shadow, which turned out to be 1½ feet, or half the length of the yardstick. Since the shadow of the flagpole was 10 feet, he calculated that the pole must be 20 feet tall.

"Max, what do you think?" Gina asked.

"I think it's easy to demonstrate how big a billion is," he replied.

"A billion what?" Tad asked

"Doesn't matter," Max shrugged.

"So, how do we do it?" pressed Gina.

"I've been thinking about it, and I think it'd be simplest if we calculated the volume of a billion marbles."

"Marbles?" Gina asked, "Why marbles?"

"Because I have a great collection of marbles," Max added, "Tomorrow, I'll have the answer."

The next day, Max had the entire plan outlined. With Gina and Tad's help, he filled a quart jar with marbles. Three hundred and ten marbles filled the jar. Simple mathematical conversions determined that one cubic foot would hold 29.92 quarts, which meant that if you multiplied 310 marbles in one quart by 29.92 quarts, you would know that there would be

9,275 marbles in each cubic foot. Thus, one billion marbles divided by 9,275 marbles required a vessel of 107,816 cubic feet. This meant that a billion marbles would completely fill a high school gymnasium.

Neville's group came up with the number of years it would take to count to a billion if you counted one number per second. As he explained to Ms. Willoughby, "There are 86,400 seconds in a day. It would take a group counting nonstop for 24 hours a day a little more than 11 days to reach a million (1,000,000 divided by 86,400 = 11.57 days), and since a billion is a thousand millions, then it would take almost 32 years to count to a billion (11.57 x 1,000 = 11,574 days divided by 365 = 31.71 years)."

Ms. Willoughby thought the concepts were imaginative, and Neville's group and Max's group nearly tied for first place. In the end, Max and his friends were awarded the first prize and Neville's group came in second. Ms. Willoughby said that Max's group won because a gymnasium full of marbles was easier to visualize than a group of people counting. Neville said nothing. He just glared at Max menacingly.

And now, not only were Max, Tad, and Gina in Florence, but so was Neville, along with a number of other students from their school.

෫෬

The class had been in Florence for two days when Dr. Kastleboro and the three friends decided to take a refreshment break. Dr. Kastleboro suggested the Rivoire, an outdoor café at the far corner of the Piazza della Signoria. They sat outside at the corner of the potted-plant-lined enclosure. Dr. Kastleboro sipped a cappuccino while the three students each enjoyed a gelato.

Beyond the café, crowds filled the piazza. The bright sun warmed the early April afternoon. On the other side of the piazza, in the shadow of the Uffizi, the major art gallery of Florence, a young man played American love songs on his electric guitar. Coins and bills filled his guitar case, and some tourists bought CDs of his music. The music was soothing and Dr. Kastleboro felt relaxed. He enjoyed the warm afternoon sun, wondering what life must have been like in this same piazza in times long past.

From their vantage point, Tad, Max, and Gina could see other touring students trying to ignore their chaperones. Amidst a plethora of languages, they watched huddled groups of older men and women struggling to decipher their guide books. On one side of the piazza, along the wall of the Uffizi, there was an open gallery of statues glorifying the centuries that comprised the Renaissance. Around them, other cafés overflowed with visitors resting and glancing at their menus.

The three middle school comrades happily and energetically chatted amongst themselves, mostly about the 17-foot copy of the famous marble statue of David, sculpted by Michelangelo, standing boldly naked above the crowd. Tad and Max were embarrassed just looking at it. Gina sensed their uneasiness and tried to appear casual, but she couldn't entirely suppress her giggles.

"Certainly a very important statue," she said, rubbing her chin in an intellectual pose, but then she broke into giggles and added, "Come on, guys, don't be embarrassed. Just appreciate the artistry."

Dr. Kastleboro explained to them that they were in the heart of a piazza that had been the center of Florentine government and politics in the Middle Ages. The city had changed very little from its Renaissance appearance due to careful preservation.

"During their lifetimes, both Leonardo da Vinci and Michelangelo Buonarroti were the artistic heroes of Florence," he said. "Leonardo was older, but after being charged in a scandal, he fled to Milan. In his absence, Michelangelo replaced him as the artist darling of Florence."

None of the students responded, far too distracted by the statue of the giant, naked man. They didn't even ask about the nature of the scandal.

As they watched, a dark cloud, out of place in the otherwise sunny sky, rolled in from the hills beyond the Arno River. The cloud brought with it a sudden, strong gust of wind. Hats and papers were blown across the piazza. Paper napkins were picked up in the wind from the outdoor cafés and flew about like white birds. Then, as quickly as they had come, the cloud and the wind were gone.

"What was that?" asked Tad.

No one answered.

In spite of the sudden wind and the noise of the surprised crowd, Gina's attention was drawn to the other side of the piazza. There, a tall man in 16th century costume caused a slight stir in the crowd. After a few minutes, she noticed the man step out of the crowd. He was broad-shouldered, and walked with a confident, athletic grace. After a few steps, the man paused, surveyed the piazza, and grinned with apparent amusement and amazement.

The man cut an impressive figure. His hair was blond with curls that ran over his ears and onto his shoulders, while his blond beard was neatly trimmed to a gentle point below his strong jaw. He was handsome with a fine, Roman nose. He wore a faded pink tunic that came to his thighs, narrow, stocking-like pants that hugged his legs, and strange slippers on his feet. Around his shoulders hung an equally faded purple cloak.

"Hey, look at that guy," said Gina, pointing across the piazza.

The group's eyes followed her finger.

"That's a reenactor playing Leonardo da Vinci," the teacher told his students.

While Dr. Kastleboro had been to Florence on many occasions, he had never seen reenactors. He wondered if the city had added this as an attraction for tourists. Perhaps he would soon see Michelangelo, Galileo, Machiavelli, and Medici, as well.

"What's a reenactor?" asked Gina.

Dr. Kastleboro explained. "A reenactor is a person, often an actor or student from an acting academy, who wears a period costume and is hired to add historical flavor to a place. For instance, at the recreated Plymouth Village in Massachusetts, an entire re-created Pilgrim village is populated with actors in period costumes. They pretend to live in that time period and claim to know nothing of the events that took place after their era."

It was at that moment that Dr. Kastleboro had an idea, a realization that fortune had just smiled upon him. *What better way to infuse my students with the essence of the Renaissance and create an interest in studying Leonardo da Vinci than by having some lessons presented by a look-alike actor?*

"Why don't I invite him to join us?" asked Dr. Kastleboro.

"That would be neat," said Max. "Maybe we can test him." He wondered if he could think of a question to trick the reenactor into revealing knowledge of some current event or, better yet, a modern contraption.

"Oh, yeah," Gina and Tad replied in unison.

"Could be fun," Dr. Kastleboro said. *Even educational,* he thought. "Okay, here's the deal. I'm going to invite him to sit with us. Then I'll suggest that he give us a little Renaissance tour of parts of this city. Whenever you can, pipe in with questions or comments to see if you can get him to reveal he is actually someone who really lives in this century."

This should be easy, thought Gina.

"Me first," shouted Tad.

"Whoever has a question, speak up any time," instructed Dr. Kastleboro.

Leaving the table, he quickly worked his way through the crowd to the actor.

As he approached the man, he noticed that the reenactor was a good foot taller than he was. He remembered that Leonardo had been described as tall, but he wondered if this actor was perhaps too tall for accuracy. In any event, Dr. Kastleboro spoke.

"*Mi scusi, posso introdurmi?* My name is Willard Kastleboro."

The man smiled and replied in Italian, "*E'un piacere fare la sua conoscenza.* Thank you for introducing yourself. It has been a long time since I have spoken to anyone. Please allow me to reciprocate. I am Leonardo da Vinci." He made a courtly bow.

Dr. Kastleboro was amazed. The reenactor's Italian was stilted, archaic, like Shakespearean English sounded to a modern American English speaker. His Italian was as if it were from an earlier era. *This guy is good*, thought Dr. Kastleboro. He smiled. "How much would it cost for some of your time? I hope to teach my students more about ancient Florence."

The Renaissance man looked strangely at him. "I would be glad to share some time in your company, good sir. No payment is necessary. In fact, I wonder why you would offer. Is it now customary to purchase someone's company? That's so peculiar. But before you answer that question, could you tell me, sir, what century this is?"

Oh, this is great, thought Dr. Kastleboro.

"The 21st, and no, it is not customary to pay someone for the pleasure of their company. I was speaking under the assumption that you had a full schedule and had no time for teenage students."

Leonardo shook his head. "I always have time for students. You say this is the 21st century? And yet so little is changed! Even the statue by that thick-headed Michelangelo is still standing," he said, nodding toward the statue of David. "However, it looks cruder than I remember."

Playing along, Dr. Kastleboro shook his head and patiently explained, "16th century Florence has been preserved for its historical significance, but Italy, and the rest of the world, is very much changed." Dr. Kastleboro knew that introducing this reenactor to his three students was going to be fun. "The statue you see is a replica of the original, which is in a museum to protect it from deterioration and pollution. I guess it was a bad idea to leave such a valuable marble statue outside."

Leonardo frowned. "It was my idea to place it here in the piazza when I was on the committee."

This was stated in the brochures in the Michelangelo Museum so it was not new to Dr. Kastleboro. He decided to get on with his plan. "Well, sir, I wonder if I can offer you some refreshment."

Leonardo looked intrigued. "I would be delighted, for it has been a long time since I last enjoyed a social drink."

"Come to our table, sir. I am sure we can answer all of your questions, and in return, you can answer ours."

The game was on.

2. THE ADVENTURE BEGINS

The students watched in fascination as the reenactor followed Dr. Kastleboro across the piazza. The man's costume was authentic. He had done a good job of looking like the real deal. As the two men approached the table, Tad, Max, and Gina rose.

"Max, Tad, Gina, our guest is the one and only Leonardo da Vinci." Dr. Kastleboro grinned as he spoke.

The students smiled in return and held out their hands for handshakes. Leonardo did not grasp their hands, but bowed instead.

"*Non conosco questa lingua,*" he said in archaic Italian, making it clear that he did not understand English. "*Ma sono lieto di apprendere la vostra conoscenza.*"

Dr. Kastleboro translated for the group. He says, "He is pleased to make our acquaintance." Then, turning back to the stranger, "*La prego di sedersi, per favore,*" gesturing to an empty chair at the table and continuing in Italian, "May I offer you a *Chinotto*?"

"I would be grateful. But, what is a *Chinotto*?" He sat down as the three students pulled their chairs closer. There was a remarkable aura around this actor. Even though none of them understood it, they all felt it.

Dr. Kastleboro smiled. He wondered how this reenactor would respond to this extremely tart orange carbonated soft drink, which obviously would be unknown to a man not from a modern century.

While his drink was being served, Dr. Kastleboro asked, *"Tu chi sei? Lei è molto, molto buono."* He was trying to find out who the gentleman was and let him know he thought he was a very good actor. Then, asking in Italian, "How did you become a Renaissance actor?"

Leonardo took a cautious sip of the dark, fizzing drink and pursed his lips at the bittersweet flavor. He answered calmly. *"Ma io non sono un attore. Io non sono in costume. Sono Leonardo da Vinci,"* he stated, letting Dr. Kastleboro know that he was neither an actor, nor in costume. He continued in Italian, "I understand your confusion. I am sure you have doubts, because for all of you, I have been dead for many centuries. But you see, I was born too soon. My birth was out of nature's ordered sequence. As a result, I was ahead of my time. I wrote down my thoughts and inventions in my notes. I was born in the 15th century and lived into the 16th century, but the centuries in which I lived were a world of wood, stone, bricks, and iron. I never had the chance to build the things I dreamed.

"Now I have a do-over, an opportunity to use my special talents for an act of importance! If I succeed, my existence will be worth more than a few pretty paintings. I am not a modest man. I know that I have vision and intelligence enough to complete a discovery or invention to change all mankind for the better."

After Dr. Kastleboro translated, the students laughed.

Tad said, "Come on, he's trying to make us look stupid."

"Looks like we need proof," responded Max, grinning.

"I agree. If you really expect us to believe something like that, you'll have to prove it," said Gina, addressing Leonardo in Italian.

The slight crinkle of his eyes showed that, even though he was frustrated by the situation, he also found it to be humorous. How would he be able to convince these people or anyone of his authenticity? He needed help to navigate this new world, but seated in this café, he didn't feel so far removed from the Florence he once knew. "I am sure my death five centuries ago makes this moment seem, well, perhaps strange. No— impossible. However, what I am telling you is true."

After Dr. Kastleboro translated, they all stared at him. This man really seemed to believe what he was saying!

"What can I do to convince you?" he added.

Tad, Max, and Gina looked at each other.

"Write backward. Your codices were written backward, so that they can only be read in a mirror," said Max.

"Do you have a quill or pen-nib and a piece of parchment?"

"No," Dr. Kastleboro answered, "but I do have a notebook and a pen from the hotel."

Taking the opened notebook, Leonardo felt the texture of the paper and studied the pen. He drew a line on the paper and then studied the pen again. "Wonderful. Such smooth and thin parchment. The writing utensil—how does it work?"

"It's called a ballpoint pen," explained Dr. Kastleboro. "A small ball presses against a cartridge of ink, causing the ink to press out on the paper as you move your pen."

"Fascinating. Do you have another?"

Gina reached into her purse and produced a second pen.

Then, without hesitation, Leonardo took a pen in each hand and swiftly sketched two horses' heads, one facing the other, each identical and each drawn at the same time, one with his left hand and one with his right. When he finished, he wrote the words "These are two twin horses with their heads facing each other." Then he spread his hands. "There," he said, looking carefully at the ballpoint pens once again.

They all stared at the drawings and the right-to-left mirror-writing. The horses' heads were beautifully proportioned and looked like many of the drawings of horses Dr. Kastleboro remembered from his studies of Leonardo da Vinci.

I wonder how he did that, thought Max.

"I am," he declared again, "really Leonardo da Vinci. Now, could you and will you direct me to someone who could help me learn enough to conceive and build or discover something new for the betterment of mankind?"

"Perhaps we can help each other," said Dr. Kastleboro.

"What was it like to be dead?" Tad cut in. Gina shot him an amused look and then translated for Leonardo. Tad shrugged and muttered to Max, "Nothing wrong with asking."

Leonardo thought about Tad's question. "To tell you the truth," he said, "I do not have any memory of being dead. I can remember the events of my life, including the moment of my death, but I have no memories of actually being dead."

Dr. Kastleboro studied the man. He could tell that his students were caught in the moment. *What lessons would they take from this adventure? This was better than Rome, better than Venice, and unquestionably better than a classroom.* "Okay," he said in Italian, deciding to play along. "Suppose, for the moment, we accept the truth of what you say. If you can answer our questions, we'll do what we can to help you with your quest."

A waiter passed by, carrying a menu. On the back, Leonardo saw a colorful photo of *zuccotto* garnished with berries, one that looked similar to a dish he had enjoyed during his first life.

"Who is the artisan? How? Such a perfect likeness. Such perfect color and scale and no brush strokes."

"No, no," said Dr. Kastleboro. "That's not a painting. It's a print from a photograph."

"A what?"

"It is a method developed to capture events and place them on paper. In your time, of course, the only way one person could capture a likeness of another was to have an artist, such as yourself, paint a portrait. That was only for the wealthy. Now, with a device known as a camera, a likeness can be captured on a piece of paper by the effect of light on chemicals."

Leonardo shook his head in wonder while Dr. Kastleboro translated the conversation to his students.

"It baffles me that something could look so real and still be an imitation." Leonardo reminisced. "I remember when I sought employment with Duke Ludovico Sforza il Moro in Milan. It was suggested that I paint a portrait of his lovely friend, Cecilia Gallerani. I had seen her reflection in a mirror and noted that when you wish to see if your painting is like the thing depicted, you take a mirror and let the living thing be reflected in it."

Leonardo pointed to the menu and stated, "However, this artist has all the skills, remarkable clarity, and perfect color, but somehow he lacks a depth of feeling."

At that moment, a group of a dozen Japanese tourists led by a tour guide carrying a small, triangular red locator flag on a long pole approached their table. "So sorry to bother you," the leader of the group said to Leonardo, "but would you mind posing for a picture?"

"Who is he?" asked an older Japanese man. "Michelangelo, Galileo, or Leonardo?"

Leonardo da Vinci looked puzzled. "What is happening? Who are these strange people? The little flag, what city-state?"

Dr. Kastleboro explained, "They are visitors to Florence. They like your costume, and they want to take your picture."

"My picture?" Leonardo questioned, picking up his drawing of the twin horses.

"Like the picture on the menu. The little boxes they are carrying are cameras that can record a picture of whatever they focus on," said Dr. Kastleboro.

"What would the people in the 16th century have done if you had a box that allowed you to make an instant picture of another person? Would they have cheered you as a great magician?" asked Gina in Italian.

As Leonardo rose to face the tourists, he chuckled and answered Gina, "I think they would have burned me as a witch. Such a device would have been frightening to the people. Most common people in the 16th century were superstitious and easily frightened by things they did not understand."

Turning to the group of tourists, he asked in Italian, "What should I do?"

"Just step out here and smile," the leader said, placing a hand on Leonardo's shoulder to guide him to stand a couple yards from the café.

The photo session only took a few minutes. When it was over, Leonardo returned to the table while the Japanese tour group excitedly clustered around their guide. After a few minutes, the group thanked Leonardo and hurried away toward the statue of David.

"What just happened?" asked Leonardo.

"Just people taking pictures," said Dr. Kastleboro.

"Some of them were taking videos," said Gina in Italian.

"What is that?"

"*Un'immagine che si muove,*" said Gina. Then, remembering to include her friends, she repeated herself in English, "A picture that moves."

Leonardo looked at them with puzzlement and wonder. "You can make a picture move?" he asked, amazed.

"Can you explain that, Max?" Gina asked after translating.

"Certainly," he said, pleased to be asked. He reached into his satchel which was hanging over his chair, and pulled out a small, yellow packet of sticky notes. "Here," he said as he drew a stickman with arms and legs in slightly different positions on each page. When he finished, he flipped the pages quickly with his thumb, causing it to appear as if the stick man was running. Leonardo watched in amazement. Max handed the packet to him.

Leonardo took the packet and flipped the pages with his thumb as Max had done, repeating it over and over. "Incredible," he said. "The speed fools the eye. But this is not movement of a picture, only the illusion of movement."

"That's right. We don't actually make a picture move. It just looks like it. Why don't you give it a try?"

After hearing Gina translate, Leonardo took the ballpoint pen and began to quickly draw on the sticky notes. His fingers flashed from one page to another, and his smile grew broader and broader as he drew, his left hand drawing while his right hand flipped the pages.

Within minutes, he was finished. He closed the pages and nodded in satisfaction. He handed the packet to Dr. Kastleboro, who flipped the pages. Impressed, he handed it to the students, who in turn flipped the pages. What they saw was a small image of the Vitruvian Man, the universal figure well recognized as the emblem of Leonardo da Vinci, appearing to wave his arms and legs.

Leonardo was happy, and he launched into an explanation. "Following the Vitruvius treatise on proportions—a man's body inscribed in a square, with his feet and arms outspread within a circle, made with its center at his navel—the artist can always get proportions correct. I learned this when my father apprenticed me to Verrocchio's studio."

"This guy is fun," said Tad after Dr. Kastleboro translated.

Max grinned. "I agree."

"What harm can it be if we help him? Maybe he has an audition and this is a test to see how good he is," said Gina in English. The reenactor was surprising and interesting, and she couldn't wait to see what else he had to show them.

"My students want to help you, Mr. da Vinci," Dr. Kastleboro told Leonardo.

"*Grazie,*" said Leonardo smiling, "*Ma per favore mi chiami Maestro.*" He continued in Italian, "Do call me Maestro, it is what everyone called me during my earlier lifetime. Where do we begin? I will need all the help I can get. I fear that, as I venture out, I will be an alien in a foreign land."

Dr. Kastleboro shook his head. He wondered if his three students, or maybe he, himself, could trick the man into revealing himself as the actor he really was. *Returning from the dead was for fiction, not real life ... right?*

3. THE AWAKENING

As Leonardo da Vinci sipped the *Chinotto*, he methodically surveyed everything around him. *What do I need to do, to learn, in order to understand this new world? How much of the knowledge I spent so much time seeking is already here? What information must I obtain in order to fulfill the requirements given to me by the gypsy woman? I need the help of these kind strangers. Will they be willing to help me? Able to help me?*

During his life in Florence, he was used to being around people who he considered ignorant. In the 15th and 16th centuries, most of the citizens of Italy could neither read nor write. Peasants in the countryside lived in cramped houses, sharing small spaces not only with each generation of the family, but also with their farm animals.

Within the city's protective walls, most of the inhabitants lived in crowded squalor, while the few who were rich and powerful lived in large, luxurious houses that were almost palaces.

In the 21st century, how are the conditions different? Can these strangers help me enough or will I need to confer with great learned men? How should I begin?

"Excuse me," he finally said. "You speak a strange language among yourselves. Where, may I ask, is your city-state or home country?"

"Siamo Americani," answered Gina.

At the mention of the name, America, Leonardo tilted his head to one side and addressed Gina. His voice revealed his intense interest. "Did you say you live in the land of America?" he asked.

"Yes," answered Gina as she pondered the question.

"And is this a land across the Atlantic Ocean?"

"Si," Gina answered, again in Italian, while Dr. Kastleboro was smiling at the exchange, "but why the question?"

"Because, our guest is a good reenactor," explained Dr. Kastleboro, speaking in English. "Now he will tell us that he was a friend of Vespucci, because they were roughly the same age and both teenagers here in Florence."

"I don't get it," said Tad, looking puzzled.

Just as Dr. Kastleboro predicted, Leonardo continued, in Italian. "We both grew up at the same time here in Florence. I was well acquainted with the Vespucci family."

Then it was true, thought Leonardo, *that Amerigo Vespucci from the city of Florence, had been right and Christopher Columbus, from the city of Genoa, had been wrong. Columbus believed that the islands he discovered sailing westward were the outer islands of India, the Indies, and that he had discovered a direct trade route to India and China; while Amerigo Vespucci who had followed in his own voyages westward, disagreed and instead believed that the land reached across the Ocean was a vast land located between Europe and the Orient. He believed that the land was, in fact, a new and previously unknown continent.*

"So, good sir," continued Leonardo, "Is it correct that there is truly a land, a continent across the Atlantic, that is between here and the Orient?"

"Yes, that's true" answered Dr. Kastleboro feeling silly telling this elementary fact to the actor.

"Then, please, tell me more of this land called America."

Gina, understanding Leonardo, turned to Dr. Kastleboro and in English asked, "What is the connection between Amerigo Vespucci and America?"

"Well," explained Dr. Kastleboro, "after the excitement created by Columbus and the story of his discovery of land across the Atlantic, Amerigo Vespucci, who was already a trained naval navigator and a map maker, began to plan his own expedition. He soon made several voyages, but his voyages did not end at the islands found by Columbus, but rather continued southward along the coast of what we now know as South America. As he explored, he mapped what he began to realize was a vast new continent.

"In describing his voyages he wrote a letter to Pier Soderini, Gonfalconier, Mayor of Florence, describing his observations. Then later, he wrote a letter to Lorenzo di Medici, his friend and mentor, also describing his voyages. These letters were well circulated and generated great excitement. There were other letters, too. A copy of some of these letters fell into the hands of Martin Waldseemuller, a clergyman with an interest in geography. He and several friends who shared his interest in geography, printed and marketed a large wall map of the world along with a book, *Cosmographiae Introducto*, which included the pamphlet by Vespucci, *Mundus Novus* (The New World). It was on this map that Waldseemuller and his friends labeled the newly discovered continent, America, in honor of Vespucci. Thus America was named and the map and the book made Vespucci famous."

"But was that fair?" pointed out Tad. "It was Columbus, not Vespucci, who first discovered America."

Dr. Kastleboro shrugged. "Life is not always fair," he said. "Still, on the other hand, Vespucci recognized that a new continent was discovered, while Columbus had not."

Leonardo listened and watched the rapid exchange in the language he could not understand.

"This America," urged Leonardo, "tell me more. I have so much to learn."

"There is a lot to tell," began Dr. Kastleboro. He then rose from the table and added, "We can discuss all these things, but first there is much we have to learn from you. May I suggest that we walk a few blocks to the Duomo? You can re-acquaint yourself with it and teach us about one of the greatest buildings of your century. Perhaps you can explain why that giant cathedral is so important to Florence. After that, we will be glad to describe the world of today."

Leonardo rose from his place at the table, nodding in agreement. "A fine idea, kind sir. Let us proceed." He couldn't help but continue to look around at the streets he knew so well. "I worked on the great globe that was hoisted onto the top of the great cathedral. The metal globe was large enough to hold a man. As people came to admire the two finished hemispheres that lay open for assembly for the crown of the building, I climbed inside the open half and pretended to be a fetus in the giant egg of Florence," he smiled.

Ms. Willoughby caught up with the group as Leonardo da Vinci, Dr. Kastleboro, Max, Tad, and Gina were getting up to leave. She had Neville Kraxton along with two girls in tow.

"Great," muttered Max. "It's Neville. There goes the fun."

"Don't worry about him," said Tad, moving around to be sure he was walking between Max and Neville.

"Who's your companion?" Ms. Willoughby asked Dr. Kastleboro, nodding at Leonardo.

"Ah, Ms. Willoughby," said Dr. Kastleboro with a smile and a wink, "our guide tells us that he is in fact the late Leonardo da Vinci returned from the dead."

"Dr. Kastleboro thinks he is a Leonardo da Vinci reenactor," said Max.

"Of course he's a fake," said Neville.

"No, not a reenactor, Max," said Ms. Willoughby. "Back home, we have reenactors in reproduced villages like Plymouth or Colonial Williamsburg, but they don't have them here in Florence. Florence is not a reproduced village. It has been preserved and is currently almost exactly as you would have seen it many centuries ago. He's just an actor."

Ms. Willoughby, almost as tall as Leonardo, looked him straight in the eyes, smiled broadly, held out her hand, and said in perfect Italian, "*E' un piacere di fare la sua conoscenza! In che teatro recita?*"

Leonardo bowed and returned her broad smile with a broader one of his own. "I know, madam," he said, "coming back from the dead does seem improbable, but it is true. I am not an actor. I am Leonardo da Vinci, brought back from the dead just this afternoon."

Max, who had been listening to Gina translate, broke in to explain. "He has been given the gift of a renewed life, and now he is going to invent or discover something for the betterment of humankind."

Ms. Willoughby laughed and, turning to Dr. Kastleboro, said, "What adventure have you planned for your guide?"

"A guided tour of the Duomo."

"Wonderful," she said, turning to check that none of the students had wandered off. "May we join you?"

4. THE BICYCLE

The group flowed out of the Piazza della Signoria and into
the Via dei Leoni, which was lined with four-story houses and
apartments. Each house had a front entrance with an arched,
eight-foot door. The windows were shuttered and a small
overhang provided protection from the rain. Even in daylight,
the narrow street was in shadow. The sidewalks on each side
of the street were not wide enough for two people to walk side
by side.

They had only walked a block when they reached the
slightly wider Piazza di San Firenze. There, a few tables and
chairs were empty outside a small café. Just beyond were rows
of bicycles standing in racks. Seeing the bicycles, Leonardo
stopped and stared.

"My double-wheeled carriers," he breathed, taking hold of
Max's arm and gripping it tightly to stop him, as well. "There
they are. Look at them. Beautiful. Even more beautiful than
I had imagined."

In the later part of the 15th century, Leonardo da Vinci had drawn a design for a bicycle. His design embraced all the details of a modern bicycle—both wheels were of the same size and driven by pedals attached to a large sprocket that moved a chain. The chain, in turn, moved a small sprocket affixed to the rear wheel. The only difference in concept was that his double-wheeled carrier was to be built entirely of wood with spokes of wooden rods for a wheel rimmed by an iron band. The "chain" was designed with leather loops.

Leonardo's face reflected his total delight at the sight of the bicycles. He remembered clearly the moment that the idea occurred to him. He had been under the employ of Ludovico Sforza il Moro, the Duke of Milan. During a city-hosted tournament, he noticed a young boy at play, rolling a wheel that had fallen from a cart. As he watched, he noted that as long as the wheel rolled, it remained upright. He quickly imagined that he could connect two wheels with a frame and a pedal with a specific gear ratio. If a man sat on top of the frame between the two wheels, he could remain balanced so long as he was moving.

Leonardo had longed to find a way to build such a machine. Unfortunately, he was unable to build it because the needed materials were never available. Now, here was his machine. He was ecstatic.

"Magnificent! It is exactly as I had envisioned. The whole concept is a mathematical marvel. Do you know what I mean?" He let go of Max, who rubbed his arm indignantly, while Leonardo waved his arms in excitement.

Ms. Willoughby laughed. "Your guide is delightful," she said to Dr. Kastleboro.

"Ummm, Max?" Gina asked, turning to her friend. "What does a bicycle have to do with math?"

Max, still rubbing his arm from where the Maestro had gripped it tightly, responded, "The speed of the bicycle is related to the gear ratio and the advantage one gear gives another."

"What?"

"The gear in the front is a big wheel sprocket connected to the pedals. The smaller gear is a wheel sprocket connected to the rear wheel. Say the wheel sprocket on the pedals has 44 teeth and the wheel sprocket on the rear has 11 teeth. Then, when the rider turns his pedals one revolution, 44 teeth will go all the way around once, while the rear wheel sprocket will have spun around four times. This means that the rear wheel is going faster than the pedals are turning. It's a simple matter of ratios: 44 to 11 or 4 to 1.

"You can also figure out the speed the bicycle is moving by using math. If we took a measuring tape and measured from one edge of the wheel through the very middle to the opposite edge of the wheel, we would have the diameter. Let's say that's 28 inches. Then, to determine the circumference, we use the formula: diameter multiplied by pi, or 3.14. So, 28 x 3.14 is…," Max paused for a moment to do the math, "87.92 inches. *Then*, if we divide that by the number of inches in a foot, 12, we know that the circumference of the wheels on a 28-inch bike is 7.33 feet."

Gina, who had been translating for Leonardo's benefit, interrupted Max. "Slow down! Trying to understand what you're saying is difficult enough without me having to figure out how to say it in Italian, too!"

Max grinned sheepishly and waited for Gina's go-ahead before he kept talking. In the meantime, he took out a notepad and started jotting down numbers. When she nodded that he could continue, he showed them his calculations and said, "Now, we're in the home stretch to figuring out how much faster it is to travel by biking than by walking. First, we need to take the ratio we calculated before—4 to 1—and multiply that by the circumference of the wheels—7.33 feet. So, each time you turn the pedals around once, the bicycle would travel 4 x 7.33 feet, or 29.32 feet, along the road. If you pedal at 60 revolutions per minute, you would go 1,759.20 feet along the road every minute. Because there are 60 minutes in an hour, then you multiply our new calculation by 60 as well to get 105,552 feet in an hour. So, now you know how many feet you can travel in an hour by biking. Next, to figure out how many miles that is, we divide 105,552 feet by 5,280—the number of feet in a mile—to get 19.99 miles traveled in an hour. That's essentially 20 miles per hour—much faster than you could walk."

Neville listened carefully to Max's explanation and then said, "Okay, Mr. Know-it-all. If you haven't noticed, we're in Italy, not America. Here they use the metric system. So, how many centimeters are there in the circumference of this 28 inch bicycle?" He smiled at his mathematical adversary, "and better still, how fast in kilometers was this bicycle going? Bet you can't figure that one."

Mathematical Max cocked his head and said, "That's simple"

"Simple to you, maybe," muttered Tad.

Max ignored this remark and continued. "We start with the basics, 2.54 centimeters equals 1 inch. If the circumference of the wheel on our 28 inch bicycle is 87.92 inches, then we multiply the 87.92 inch circumference by 2.54 centimeters and arrive at ...," he paused while he thought, "223.32 centimeters."

"How about the speed?"

"That's even easier. We have already decided that the bike will be traveling at approximately 20 miles per hour. We know that 1 mile is 1.61 kilometers, so we multiply 20 times 1.61 and determine that the bike is traveling at the rate of 32.2 kilometers per hour, or, more simply, at a speed of about 32 kilometers per hour. Not all numbers are that easy, of course, but we can round them to make quick calculations.

"We all know that when people talk about running a 5K race, they mean 5 kilometers, which most understand is roughly 3 miles plus a little. Our imaginary bicycle was travelling at around 20 miles per hour, so we divide by 3 and multiply by 5 to get our kilometers. So, 20 divided by 3 equals 6.67 multiplied by 5 we get 33.35. That means the bicycle travels at about 33 kilometers per hour. While not as accurate as our earlier calculation, it is close enough for approximations. So, if we keep that simple ratio in mind, merely divide by 3 and multiply by 5, it is always easy to make a simple, crude, no-paper-needed conversion."

"Wow, Max," said Gina, "you did all that in your head?"

"Humph," muttered Neville, rolling his eyes.

"Now," continued Max, ignoring Neville, "if you are using a 10-speed or even a 24-speed bike, there are a lot more gear-ratio combinations to consider."

"I think you've explained enough, Max," Tad interrupted with a grin. He was well acquainted with Max's explanations and knew that he could keep talking for at least another hour.

Leonardo dropped to his knees to look more closely at the bicycle. "The materials. How extraordinary! And the wheels. Soft, yet strong. What is it?"

"That's rubber," Dr. Kastleboro explained. "Rubber is an elastic, flexible, tough material fabricated from the sap of a rubber tree. Here, it forms a pneumatic tube."

"Excuse me?"

"Pneumatic. It means that the rubber tube, or tire, is filled with air for a faster, softer, smoother ride."

"What are these two-wheeled carriers called?"

"Bicycles."

"Are they used by many people?"

"Millions and millions, all over the world," said Dr. Kastleboro, wondering if this actor was enjoying the joke of feigning total bewilderment. He was so genuine, though, that he could only be admired.

Leonardo was astonished. "Millions?" If people throughout the world were using his invention, then he had already invented something for the betterment of mankind! He turned to Dr. Kastleboro. "How long has my machine been used?"

"Sorry, Maestro, but it is not actually your machine."

"But my design?"

"Unfortunately for humankind, your codices were lost for many centuries after your death. You must remember that you left all of your notebooks with your assistant, Francesco Melzi. Well, he tried to organize them, but he never finished. When he died, his family gave them away, and soon, they vanished. It was several centuries before many of your notebooks were discovered. The one with your bicycle drawing wasn't discovered until your *Codex Atlanticus* was being restored in the middle of last century.

"No one was even aware of your design when the bicycle was invented. The first practical bicycle was built out of wood with metal wheels in 1865. In that design, the front wheel was larger than the back wheel and the pedals turning the big front wheel were connected directly to the wheel itself. Obviously, the larger the wheel, the more distance covered with each revolution and the faster the bicycle could go. So people kept making the front wheels bigger and bigger. By 1870, the bicycle was made entirely out of metal with solid rubber tires. It took another generation to develop a bicycle like the ones you see here—like the one you designed. Your concept was correct, but it wasn't seen until long after the bicycle as we know it was invented."

Leonardo ran his hands over the machine, testing the texture of the black plastic seat, the metal frame, and the rubber tires. He studied the chain. "*Fantastico*! It is almost exactly as I envisioned. And the materials! How wonderful ..."

At that moment, a young man in his late teens or early twenties came out of a café and approached the group. His hair was long, and he wore an oversized denim jacket, low-slung pants, and a backward Dodgers baseball cap.

"Hey, whatcha doing with my bike?" he said in Italian. Gina responded first. "*Niente, niente.* Our friend was just admiring it. Believe it or not, he's never ridden a bike."

"It's a beautiful machine," said Leonardo.

"Yeah. Hey, you kiddin'? Never rode a bike before?" he asked.

"They didn't exist when I grew up."

"Man, what century you been living in?"

"You have no idea," mumbled Gina, rolling her eyes.

"You seem kinda cool," said the boy. Then he added, pointing to Leonardo's leggings, tunic and cape, "Look, *Signore*. I like your gig. I'm thinking about acting, too, when I finish school. Look, if you'd like to give the bike a try, I'll show you how."

The kid removed the bike from the rack. "Hop on," he said.

"When I give you a push, you've got to pedal to keep your speed and balance. And it is important to remember... ".

54

Before he could finish, Leonardo was astride the bike.
"Tell him about the brakes!" insisted Max.
Gina quickly stepped up to the Maestro and said, "The brakes to stop the bike are on the handle." She pointed to the two brake levers. "Squeeze the right one for the rear wheel and the left one for the front wheel," and she demonstrated. "But be sure to squeeze the right one first."

Before any more could be said, the young man gave Leonardo a hard push. The bike and rider went flying down the narrow street, his purple cloak flapping behind him like a fluttering flag and the bicycle wobbling dangerously. "The right handle first!" shouted Gina.

"*Vai! Vai!*" the kid hollered with great enthusiasm.

The Maestro raced down the dark street, swinging erratically from side to side toward the far corner. The owner of the bike removed his cap and beat it against his hand as he whooped, howled, and laughed at the unfolding scene. People along the street turned and watched. Someone began to snap photos of this tall, bearded man in Renaissance costume as he wobbled down the street.

Suddenly, there was a loud blast from a car horn as a black Citroën roared around the corner. Leonardo and the bicycle were squarely in the middle of the street. The driver of the Citroën swerved to the right as Leonardo gripped both brake handles at the same time. The bicycle stopped abruptly, and the man who had painted the *Last Supper* and the *Mona Lisa* flew into the air, his legs outstretched like a great bird of prey, sprawled on the hood of the car.

The owner of the bike whooped even harder. The man with the video camera continued recording, and the rest of the group rushed to the accident scene.

The driver of the Citroën leaped from his car, incredulous. "*Ma che sei pazzo?!*"

"Are you all right?" shouted Dr. Kastleboro as he ran down the street.

As the crowd gathered at the site, Leonardo slowly slid from the hood, stood upright and looked intrigued. "I've suffered no harm, but what form of cart did I land on?"

Just beyond the Arno, there was a flash of lightening followed closely by a clap of thunder.

Unseen by the others, the kid rushed to the scene, pushed through the gathering crowd and picked up his bicycle. "This was fun," he said as he mounted it and rode off. He quickly disappeared back up the street.

At the same time a police officer appeared. "*Che succede?*"

"I'll tell you what happened," said the Citroën driver. "This idiot was riding a bike down the middle of the street. I almost hit him coming around a corner."

"Where is the bike?" asked the officer.

It was then that they all noticed that the bike and owner were gone. Dr. Kastleboro tried to explain. Pointing to Leonardo, he said, "He was riding a bike when the car came around the corner. Fortunately, they were both able to stop before any serious damage could happen."

The policeman looked at Leonardo. "Hey, what's the costume for? Are you a vendor? What are you selling? Do you have a vendor permit? Where's your booth?"

Leonardo was confused—he had hoped his fame had lasted. "I am Leonardo da Vinci," he replied.

The officer laughed. "Yeah, and I'm the Pope. Let me see your I.D."

Leonardo raised an eyebrow. He was almost certain that this man was not the Pope. His dress and manner were all wrong.

Dr. Kastleboro, Ms. Willoughby, and all the students pressed in closer. Now the actor's real identity would be revealed.

"I'm afraid, sir, I don't understand."

The police officer was uncertain about the man's strange Italian accent. "Identification. A driver's license, a passport, a credit card or, better yet, your vendor's permit."

The group watched.

"I am sorry, but I do not understand."

"Papers. Papers. Where are your papers?"

The scene was attracting more and more people. Apparently, a man in Renaissance costume and a police officer meant excitement. From behind the Citroen, a heavy-set man with dark hair rimming a bald head pushed through the crowd. He was carrying a microphone and chewing the stump of a cigar. Beside him, a trimmer man with a television camera resting on his shoulder filmed the spectacle.

"*Certo, si va bene signor vigile,*" said the man with the microphone to the police officer, offering a broad smile. "He is one of our actors. We're doing a commercial."

The policeman frowned, shrugged, and said, "Yeah? Well, don't film in the middle of the street next time. This is not a studio."

As the police officer left and the driver sped off, the television man turned to Leonardo. "I'm Antonio Gigliardi, *Canale 10 Firenze*, Director of Human Interest Stories. That's quite a costume. What's your gig?" He handed Leonardo his card.

Jerking his thumb toward his assistant, Antonio said, "He's Joseph—Joe. Great cameraman."

"I am afraid I do not understand. Did I do something wrong?" asked Leonardo. "Was His Holiness concerned about my falling on the black cart?"

While they were talking, Max turned to Tad and Gina and said, "If he's genuine, then he's about to get caught up in a television story."

Gina nodded and added, "And he'll never get to achieve his goal. We need to get him out of here."

The teachers, listening to their conversation, interjected.

"No," said Ms. Willoughby. "We need to watch and find out who he is before we do anything more."

Meanwhile, Leonardo was telling the media director, "In full honesty, my last place of residence was the Manor at Cloux, but mostly, I have been dead."

Antonio and Joe looked at each other and smiled. Joe kept filming. "Dead, huh? Well, look, *Signor da Vinci...*"

"Most people call me Maestro."

"Maestro, then. Well, you're very much alive right now. If that car had been going a little faster, though, you could have died for a second time!" Antonio was trying hard not to laugh. "But, listen, I have an offer for you."

"What is it?"

"You've got a great costume. A perfect beard. A nice face. You look authentic. And if you want to insist you're the real da Vinci, that's fine with me. Maybe even better. We can pay you well," continued Antonio Gigliardi. "We'll get you one of those color-by-number posters of the *Mona Lisa* they sell in the gift shops, set up an easel for you in our studio, and if you follow the numbers, you can paint a new *Mona Lisa* every night on television while you tell stories about old Renaissance Florence. You'll be a hit."

Leonardo was puzzled. "I'm not sure I understand your offer of employment, but I must decline, for I have no time. I have a quest to pursue."

"Quest? Are you da Vinci or Don Quixote?"

Joe laughed. "Good. Very good, Tony."

Small drops of rain began to sprinkle the group. While Leonardo spoke with Antonio, the three friends talked quietly amongst themselves.

"There's something about this man that makes me want to believe him," Gina said.

"Well, he definitely *looks* like the real deal," Tad responded, looking Leonardo up and down. "What do you think, Max?"

Max was thoughtful. He analyzed what he knew of Leonardo da Vinci and compared it with this man they had just met that afternoon. Could he be the real deal? Finally, Max nodded and said, "I don't know, guys. We'll just have to pay attention. You remember the scientific process? For now, let's go with the hypothesis that Leonardo is the real deal. Then, if we see no evidence to the contrary and everything points to that hypothesis being right, we'll know."

"Sounds good to me," said Tad. He was never one to think too hard about something once he had already made a decision about it. Max's idea made sense to him, so he immediately accepted it.

Gina, on the other hand, turned to Max and pointed out, "Okay that's fine but it doesn't tell us what to do now. If this man really is Leonardo da Vinci, he's about to get caught up in being a celebrity, and then he won't have time to invent or discover *anything*."

"So, what should we do?" asked Tad.

"I'm not sure," said Max. He wasn't finished thinking it through that far.

Before they could come up with anything, a sudden rush of wind swept down the narrow street and a torrent of rain washed over all of them. People began to run toward shelter. The wall of water that plummeted from the sky created a momentary curtain.

"Come on!" yelled Tad, always the quickest of the three to take action. He grabbed Leonardo's arm and started to pull him towards cover.

Max and Gina were right behind them.

Gina shouted, "Hurry, Maestro! Come with us!"

Leonardo felt sure that the adults did not believe he could have returned from death, but then he probably wouldn't have believed it himself. He wasn't sure why, but he trusted the three kids.

Without hesitation, he allowed himself to be drawn away from the center of the street. People were racing in every direction to escape the downpour. Tad led them around the corner into the Via degli Speziali, leaving their school group behind. Still running, the four entered the broad Piazza della Repubblica.

"The Maestro can never reach his goal if he remains in 16th century clothes. He needs a disguise," Tad shouted to his friends. "Gina, can you tell him that we're going to try to get him into dry, modern clothes?"

Leonardo nodded when Gina explained. Then she added her own instruction, "And Maestro, you have to stop telling people you're Leonardo da Vinci. You sound like a nutcase."

Leonardo frowned and nearly came to a stop. "A nutcase?" he asked, looking confused.

Tad groaned, pulling on his arm again to keep him moving.

5. THE DEPARTMENT STORE

The three friends and Leonardo stood looking at the series of stores along the perimeter of the Piazza della Repubblica. Within the large piazza were row upon row of booths similar to the ones they had passed earlier. Brightly colored banners hung from wires high above the booths. It was a festival of activity and the vendors were removing the plastic covers they had hastily thrown over their merchandise for protection from the sudden storm. Max spotted La Ranascenta, a modern department store in the middle of the buildings, rimming the ancient center of old Florence.

"In there," Max said, pointing to the store.

Leonardo didn't move. "Wait," he said. "That shiny, black horseless cart I crashed into—what was it?"

Gina answered. "It was an automobile. A truly horseless vehicle. It's powered by a gasoline engine."

Leonardo shook his head. He did not understand what she was saying. "Gasoline engine?" he repeated.

Gina translated for Max and Tad.

Tad responded. "No. No, Gina. I can explain, but not now. Right now we have to get Maestro out of his 16th century clothes. People are staring."

Leonardo nodded in agreement when Gina explained. "Please proceed," he said.

With their clothes soaked and clinging to them, they hurried along the street to the department store and pushed open the large glass entrance doors.

"What is this place?" asked Leonardo.

"*Un grande magazzino*," said Gina. "It's a large market place."

He stopped and stared at what was before him, looking all around, trying to absorb the wonders. Bright fluorescent lights filled the building with what seemed like the brightness of the sun. There were glass counters and cabinets, each lit from the inside and filled with perfumes, jewelry, watches, and devices he could not identify. Nearby were racks of clothes and shelves containing purses and shoes with strange shapes and sizes in a painter's palate of colors. A pleasant smell wafted through the store. Though he couldn't see any musicians, a soft and unfamiliar music surrounded him. For the first time, Leonardo did not feel like he was in Florence. This place seemed magical, other-worldly.

The three teenagers and the 16th century man dripping water on the shiny, marble-like floor quickly drew the attention of the manager. She was a matronly lady, who descended toward them on the central escalator with a scowl on her face.

Leonardo watched the escalator in fascination. "What form of human locomotion is that?" he wondered aloud.

Gina laughed. "She's coming down on an escalator. Come see." She led Leonardo closer to the moving steps.

"Amazing," he exclaimed once they were close enough to examine them. "Stairs that glide. But where do they disappear to?"

While the four stood at the base of the escalator, the manager reached the bottom and stepped from the platform.

Assuming they were American, she addressed them in English. "My, aren't we the wet ones? I am quite certain that this is *not* the right store for the four of you. Perhaps I can direct you somewhere more appropriate," she said with a tight smile.

"There are some nice booths just across the piazza. Or you

can go to the San Lorenzo Market on the streets around the San Lorenzo Church on the Piazza Madonna degli Aldobrandini, just a few blocks past the Duomo."

Gina ignored the manager's rude tone and said simply, "We want to buy a dry set of clothes for our friend, please."

"I'm sure you would be perfectly pleased with the selection at another store."

Leonardo, without understanding exactly what they were saying, could tell there was tension because of the expressions on their faces. "If my presence is a problem, perhaps I can explain," he said in his archaic Italian as he stepped forward between his companions and the manager.

"No," cut in Gina. "No." Then, turning to Leonardo, she whispered in Italian, "Please, Maestro, no more with the Leonardo da Vinci. The purpose of new clothes is to hide your identity. You'll never attain your goal if you remain a celebrity, or worse, a sideshow."

As they spoke, Leonardo's attention was directed elsewhere. What kind of force allowed for such artificial light to flow through this store? What was the engine of power that propelled the horseless cart he had landed on? What allowed the stairs to move people up and down? It was exciting—and he needed to know. Would these youngsters be able to explain it all to him, or did he need the help of someone more educated?

Before he could ask, Ms. Howdershell pushed into the store. Seeing the three students with a tall stranger dressed in a Renaissance costume, wet and confronting what appeared to be a store manager, she guessed there was trouble.

Gina saw their science teacher first and rushed to her side. "Ms. Howdershell, I'm glad you are here. We have a problem. We need to buy some clothes for Maestro." She nodded toward Leonardo.

"What in the world?" exclaimed the teacher. "Where are Ms. Willoughby and Dr. Kastleboro? You shouldn't be wandering around—"

"Are you responsible for these teenagers?" interrupted the manager, turning angrily to Ms. Howdershell.

Before she could answer, the door opened again, this time by Dr. Kastleboro and Ms. Willoughby, both of whom were followed closely by Neville and the other students.

"There," said Neville, "I told you they ran down this street with the impersonator."

Ms. Howdershell quickly pulled Dr. Kastleboro aside. "Do you know anything about this man the kids want to buy clothes for?"

Dr. Kastleboro, relieved to have found the students, shrugged. "Only that he was acting as our guide. He claims to be Leonardo da Vinci, the original, reincarnated."

Ms. Howdershell suppressed a laugh. "The what?"

Meanwhile, a small cluster of customers had stopped their shopping to watch the strange activity at the foot of the escalator. Customers coming down the escalator paused at the bottom to join the spectators.

"I want you all out of my store. I'm sure your business will be more appreciated elsewhere," the manager said archly to the teachers, glancing uneasily at the growing crowd. She left them momentarily to do some crowd control, doing her best to herd customers back to their shopping. Her efforts were mostly ignored.

"Please, Dr. Kastleboro," said Max, interrupting his teachers' hushed conversation. "We need to get the Maestro out of his Renaissance clothes. He needs to look like us so he can learn enough about the 21st century to reach his goal."

Ms. Howdershell turned to Max. "What are you talking about?"

Max, Tad and Gina tried to explain, but they talked so fast, and all at the same time, that it was difficult for their science teacher to make out their tale. Finally, Tad shushed his friends.

"Ms. Howdershell, we believe this man is the late Leonardo da Vinci. He has been allowed to return to life so he can discover or invent something for the benefit of mankind. He couldn't do it in the past because they didn't have TV or phones or cars or anything that he could work with. There's a good chance that he is the real deal. Look." He showed the science teacher the drawing that Leonardo had made. While the drawing was water-soaked and smeared, the twin facing horses' heads and the mirror-writing were still impressive.

She studied the drawing and then looked over at Tad, searching his eyes. She finally said, "It's an impressive drawing, Tad, and he obviously has a lot of talent, but this can't be Leonardo da Vinci. There just isn't any scientific evidence to support the theory of reincarnation, or time travel, for that matter."

Meanwhile, cameras were flashing as some of the spectators exercised their rights as tourists to take pictures of anything that looked historic or interesting.

"He's kinda soaked," said someone from the crowd, "but he does look like a younger version of that Leonardo statue by the Uffizi."

The manager returned and impatiently said, "This is all nonsense. Would you all please take this show out into the piazza!"

Dr. Kastleboro addressed the store manager. "S*ignora, per piacere*. Before we attract any more attention, let me see if I can sort this out." Turning to Leonardo, he said in Italian, "I'm surprised that you didn't take advantage of the TV attention, which I assumed, as an actor, was what you wanted."

"No, I—"

Dr. Kastleboro continued, "Whatever your game is, you can't have these students buying you clothes. They don't have money to buy you clothes."

Leonardo drew himself straight and tall. After all, he was Leonardo da Vinci, renowned artist and personal friend of King Francis of France. "Dr. Kastleboro, with all due respect, that is not it at all," he said. "You completely misunderstand. I am not a stage actor pretending to be Leonardo da Vinci. *I am Leonardo da Vinci!*" he raised his voice. "And I did not ask these children to buy clothes for me. I have enough money to make the purchase myself." He reached beneath his wet cloak and produced 14 gold coins.

When he handed them to Dr. Kastleboro, the teacher gasped. "Why, they look just like 16th century Florentine gold florins!"

The store manager watched in amazement. Those nearby pressed closer to look at the bright, golden coins.

"Here, let me see," said Ms. Howdershell. She inspected both sides and bounced them in her hand to test their weight. They certainly had the hefty weight of gold. As she handed them back to Dr. Kastleboro, he said, "Amazing! Students, the gold florin was the standard coinage in Medici Florence." He was unable to hide his excitement. "I've only seen one of these in a museum. Look at this." He showed them to the students and even the store manager.

On the front of each of the coins was the *fleur-de-lis* badge of the city of Florence, an arching swirl flowing on both sides of a graceful pedestal. On the back was St. John the Baptist, holding a staff diagonally across his chest. "If these are real, they are quite valuable. They are certainly worth at least a thousand dollars each—probably more."

"Probably a lot more," volunteered a stranger.

"Then each one would be worth at least 1,164,000 lire," said Max, making a quick mental calculation.

"How do you figure that?" asked Neville. "I didn't see you use a calculator."

"I don't need a calculator. It's easy. Just calculate the exchange rates. One American dollar is equal to 1,164 lire on today's lire-dollar exchange. So, if gold florins are worth $1,000, we just multiply $1,000 times 1,164 lire and get 1,164,000 for each gold florin."

"Then how much are 14 florins worth?" asked Gina.

"Easy," said Max, "1,164 multiplied by 14 is 16,296,000 lire."

"Hey, Mr. Smart Guy, Europe has switched to the Euro," pointed out Neville, unhappy because he considered himself "The Great Math Student."

"You're almost right, Neville," said Dr. Kastleboro. "Euros were approved last year, but they won't be switching here for another couple years. These things take time."

"Well, it's enough for him to buy clothes," Gina cut in.

"Is the florin still the coin of Florence?" asked Leonardo, not following the exchange in English. "Each should be worth at least six lire or 120 soldi."

"It's worth considerably more than that," said Dr. Kastleboro, translating for the others. "I'm only guessing at the value of a 16th century gold florin. It doesn't look worn or old. It's in mint condition. Someone needs to find a numismatic store to have it appraised."

"Numismatic? What's that?" asked Tad.

"Where they buy or sell rare coins, doofus," said Neville, smirking at Tad.

Turning to Leonardo, Ms. Howdershell asked, "These are not stage props. How did you get these coins?"

"Why, *Signora*, I brought them with me," he said.

"From where?"

"France."

"France?"

"Yes. I had them with me when I died." He smiled.

"It looks like we will be buying clothes after all," Dr. Kastleboro said, turning to the store manager.

She nodded curtly and managed a polite smile. "Let me know if I can be of any help," she said, leaving them to help another customer who was looking at a case of expensive perfumes.

Dr. Kastleboro turned back to the group. "For now, we'll put it on my credit card. I'm sure that these gold florins are worth more than enough to cover some very nice clothes."

The crowd started to disperse now that the excitement was over.

"If that's your plan, okay," said Ms. Howdershell.

"The rain has stopped, so I'll take my group and get back to the real world. We've got some bargain hunting to do on the piazza."

"Good," said Dr. Kastleboro. "I'll take care of Leonardo da Vinci." He nodded toward Gina, Max and Tad. "As for you three, I want you to go back to the hotel and get into dry clothes. After I get new clothes for our Maestro, we'll find a place here in the piazza to wait. Come back and find us, and we'll see if we can get a handle on the truth."

"Later, with your permission," he said as he turned to Leonardo and continued in Italian, "I'll take the gold florins to the Galleria dell'Accademia—someone there can probably help." Dr. Kastleboro knew that even if the coins were counterfeit, they probably still had value because they were a great imitation. Only real gold or lead coated with gold could weigh that much. But counterfeit or not, they certainly were worth the price of a few clothes. If they weren't counterfeit, well, there had to be a logical explanation as to how this actor could be in possession of the gold florins.

Before they left, Dr. Kastleboro whispered to Ms. Willoughby, "I'm curious about how handy he is with a zipper. It wasn't developed for clothing until 1937, and that's where I may trick the truth from our man." Then Dr. Kastleboro turned and said, "Let's go find the men's section, Maestro. It looks like we've got some shopping to do."

Max had overheard Dr. Kastleboro's comment. As they left the store, he said quietly to Tad and Gina, "Looks like Dr. Kastleboro will become famous for being the man who showed the great Leonardo da Vinci, hero of the Renaissance, how to zip his fly."

The three laughed as they hurried toward the hotel.

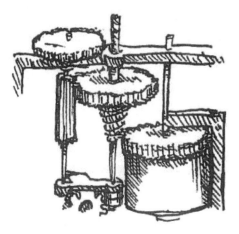

6. THE AFTERNOON

Leonardo, Dr. Kastleboro, Ms. Willoughby and Neville found an empty table beneath the wide, red umbrellas of the Café Grilli in front of the beige-brick Hotel Olimpa. The newly clad Leonardo toyed with the buttons and pockets of his khakis and the zipper of his new, dark brown leather bomber jacket. Fascinated with the zipper on the jacket, he continuously moved it up and down.

"I like these modern clothings," Leonardo said. "I think I like the pockets and the fasteners best. Practical and handy. And this zipper—precise metal work. It was nice of you to costume me in the new fashion."

Like it or not, the alleged Leonardo da Vinci had become a central part of this visit to Florence. Dr. Kastleboro realized that Max, Gina, and Tad were convinced that they had to help Leonardo find a way to satisfy his so-called quest.

Responding to Leonardo's thank you for the clothes, Dr. Kastleboro smiled and replied, "Well, Maestro, if you're serious about learning to live in the 21st century, we certainly couldn't let you go about looking like you belong in the 16th."

Leonardo agreed with him, and for the first time all day, no one seemed to pay attention to them as they sat at the café.

When the waiter approached to take their order, Leonardo had to be instructed on how to request food, something he found mildly embarrassing, since he could see that everyone around him already knew how to do so. On top of that, he could tell Dr. Kastleboro was not taking him seriously. He knew he had to say something.

After the waiter left, Leonardo began, "Remember in the department store, we passed an area where they were selling what you told me were television sets. There, shining through glass, were pictures of people moving and talking. You told me those pictures were of events taking place at that very moment in some other location, that those pictures traveled from the other place through the air as invisible waves and into that device. The idea that a picture and a sound could travel through air and appear on the glass of a box seems as impossible to me as my returning from death must seem to you.

"If I had owned this kind of device during the 16th century and shown it to the citizenry of Florence, I would have been labeled a witch, imprisoned, and burned at the stake. As I explained earlier, people were highly superstitious and feared anything that was unknown or that they could not understand. So, why do you all question or fear something you do not understand or cannot explain?"

After a moment, Dr. Kastleboro replied, "We understand the science that allows signals of sound and sight to travel invisibly through the air in waves. On the other hand, we do not know any basis upon which the dead can rise."

"Fair enough," said Leonardo. "But my situation is the only mystery to you, while both that and the television sets are mysteries to me." He paused. "Now, if you would please enlighten me. The word 'electricity' seems to play a role in this force that allows so many things to happen. The car and the television sets suggest to me that I might find my quest in a new development for the use of electricity, whatever that might be. Perhaps—"

He was interrupted as Gina, Tad, and Max arrived in a flurry of energy, running across the piazza. They grabbed chairs from a nearby empty table and crowded around Leonardo. Ms. Howdershell and the rest of the students were all walking along the other side of the piazza. Dr. Kastleboro waved at her and she returned the wave with a smile, but did not join them.

Earlier, after Max, Tad, and Gina changed clothes, they gathered in the tiny lobby of the hotel and discussed what plan they could develop to determine, once and for all, whether Leonardo was the real deal or not.

"Let's quiz him about the Black Plague. Let's see if he can provide details historians have overlooked," Gina had suggested. The idea was unanimously agreed upon, and now it was up to Gina to put it into action.

They had barely caught their breath before she said, "Hey, Maestro, we've all been wondering, were you around here during the Plague? The time of the Black Death, that is."

"The Black Death," he shuddered. He paused as he began to recall. "Yes, but not here in Florence. It lasted on and off for hundreds of years. Why do you ask about it? Do you mean to tell me it is gone?"

"Well, it's not exactly gone," said Dr. Kastleboro. "A few individual cases appear from time to time, but no epidemics. It's not important now because it can be easily cured."

"*Grazie al cielo!*" exclaimed Leonardo, his face breaking into a large, relieved smile. He then started to tell them about the disease, speaking slowly and in an instructive tone. While he spoke, Gina translated for her friends.

"The Plague first came to the Italian peninsula over a hundred years before I was born. I was told that it arrived on merchant ships as they sailed into port in Genoa in the fall of 1347. These were the same merchant ships that carried trades-men to the walled city of Caffa in Crimea. At that time, Muslims, under the leadership of a local ruler named Kipchak khan Janbeg, had blockaded the Christian merchants in Caffa, a walled city, and were planning an attack on the city. Kipchak khan Janbeg wanted to kill all of the Christians. Just as he was about to mount his attack, his men began to fall ill with a myste-rious disease. Within days, large numbers of his soldiers died.

"He blamed the Christian merchants hiding behind the walls of the city for the death of his soldiers. In great anger, he catapulted the bodies of his dead soldiers over the walls into the city before ending the siege. The bodies brought the disease inside the walls, where it spread wildly. To escape the danger, the merchants fled to the safety of their ships and the sea.

"These were the ships of Genoa's merchant fleet that regularly travelled to the Crimean region of Eastern Europe. In Genoa, it was expected that the merchants and their ships would bring exciting new things from Caffa, such as spices, silks, and objects of art, and the sailors from the ships would tell tales of the wonders of the mysterious places of the East."

Leonardo's expression grew sad as he began to recall the fear and anxiety created by the Black Death. A modern cure did nothing to assuage the pain the Plague caused in the past. The students were fascinated by what he was saying, and even the teachers listened intently.

"Instead, what they found was an unbelievable horror. Some of the ships did not make it into port because all of the crew and the merchant passengers died, leaving their ships abandoned and adrift at sea. These abandoned ships became ghost ships, garrisoned by a crew of grotesque corpses as the vessels drifted endlessly in the rolling sea, battered by storms until they sank. No one dared approach them. The few ships that did make it to port and reached the docks were found to be manned by men who were sick and dying, standing shakily amidst their dead shipmates. Even the living looked like walking skeletons, their faces covered with black and blue splotches with oozing, bulbous growths and pus-filled sores."

"Yuck," said Gina in English, but continued to translate.

"When the city officials saw the crews, they refused to allow the sailors or the merchants to leave their ships. Instead, they were left to die on their vessels. But even with that quarantine, the Black Death came ashore anyway and spread like a raging fire through the city, then to other cities and towns in the countryside and, from there, up into all of Europe.
It struck everyone, rich and poor. After a time, its ravages subsided, and then, without warning, it returned again with its cruel rage."

"Were you scared?" asked Gina, mesmerized by the tale.

"Scared? Yes. We all feared the Black Death; it was terrible. I was living in Milan when the Plague struck that city. I saw many of my friends and neighbors ..." Leonardo's narrative trailed off.

After a moment, he looked into the faces of his audience, took a deep breath to steady himself, and continued. "Usually, a person with the Plague would die within a week. Sometimes, they would be perfectly well in the morning and be dead by nightfall. Once struck by the Black Death, the glands in the neck, armpits and groin would swell, quickly growing to the size of an egg. Next, dark splotches appeared on their skin, followed by great boils oozing with pus. A foul smell emanated from their bodies as if they were rotting, like spoiled meat.

"Their minds began to fail as they were gripped by a raging fever, causing them to gyrate wildly, screaming and spinning while shouting words no one could understand. We called these terrible fits the dance of death because at the end of the dance they would fall to the ground and die in a pool of putrid fluids. No one knew what caused the Black Death or why it would come and why it would go."

"What did you do?" Max asked, his unblinking stare focused on the Maestro.

Leonardo listened as Gina translated, then responded, "Do? Nothing. What could we do? Many thought that it came from evil vapors. Others thought it was brought about by the Jews as an attack on the good Christian people. I personally felt that it had something to do with the filth that people lived in. In most cities, those in poverty often threw their waste out of their windows and into the street to be removed by street cleaners, or they dumped their waste into open ditches that flowed to the rivers. People lived in grimy, crowded buildings.

"Every morning, men would come with wagons, calling out for the dead to be brought out and put in the cart. The bodies were taken to a mass burial place or were burned in fire pits. I noticed that more people were dying of the Black Death in the city than in the country. As quickly as I could, I gathered my entourage, my assistants and servants, and fled from Milan into the countryside, where we remained until all traces of the Plague were gone. Over a third of the people of Milan died from the Black Death."

Leonardo paused, the air around them heavy.

Gina broke the silence first. "Did you ever learn what caused the Plague?"

"No, we never did. Is it something you understand in the 21st century?"

Dr. Kastleboro answered, speaking each sentence in Italian first and then in English. "We have learned that the disease was carried to Italy by infected black rats that came from East Asia. They traveled secretly with the caravans that were travelling the Silk Road out of China, and across India to the Crimean port cities. The rats then hid on the ships that were travelling from the Black Sea to Italy. While the sailors and merchants were barred from leaving their ships to come ashore, these rats left the ships by running along the ropes tying the ships to the docks. The rats then made their new home in the houses and shops in Genoa and some found their way to the other cities of Italy and then up into the rest of Europe.

"The rats carried bacteria named *Yersinia pestis*. The rats also carried fleas. When the fleas bit the rats, they became infected with the bacteria. When one of those fleas bit a person, that person became infected with the bacteria and thus contracted the Plague. If an infected person coughed, sneezed, or touched someone else, they too could become infected. It was extraordinarily infectious and spread rapidly. Today, good sanitation removes any great infestation of black rats, and the Plague, if diagnosed early, is treatable with antibiotics."

"Well," said Leonardo, fascinated by the explanation, "I understand most of what you said, except for 'bacteria' and 'antibiotics'?"

Dr. Kastleboro nodded and said, "We'll have to ask Ms. Howdershell later for a full answer. I can give you a general idea, but first, what is your current understanding of medicine, Maestro?"

Leonardo responded, while Dr. Kastleboro provided the translation. "I have long believed that the commonly accepted beliefs were wrong, but try as I might, I could never figure out what was right." He slowly sipped his *Chinotto* and tried to assemble his thoughts. "In my lifetime, the accepted belief was in the theory of humors. It had been so for over a thousand years."

"You mean everybody laughing?" asked Tad, smiling, and Gina translated.

"No," said Leonardo, returning the smile with amusement. "And by your comment, I assume that the public no longer believes in the theory. It was called humoralism—meaning that the human body was held in balance by four basic fluids: red blood, black bile, yellow bile, and phlegm. Those were the four humors. Good health meant that the four fluids were in balance. When there was too little of any one of these humors, a person became sick.

"The idea of four humors is very much akin to the four elements: earth, fire, water, and air; earth being predominant in black bile, fire in yellow bile, water in phlegm, and all of them present in red blood. As a result, many cures for illness involved cutting into a vein to let the patient bleed, which we called 'bloodletting.' It was supposed to bring the body's humors back into balance. Other methods involved various herbs and magical mixtures. I always thought that bleeding a sick person caused more death than recovery, but I could never learn enough to question the practices doctors had relied upon for over a thousand years. It was the accepted wisdom of the day. So now you can tell me that I was right, and that humoralism was wrong," he grinned.

"*Maestro, lei aveva ragione*," said Dr. Kastleboro, assuring him that he was, indeed, correct.

Then he turned to Max, Gina, and Tad and said in English, "Ms. Howdershell told me earlier this week that you just finished a science section on microbes. Why don't you three explain what microbes and antibiotics are to the Maestro?"

"Wow," said Tad. "I'm glad I don't speak Italian. Looks like it's up to you, Gina." Seeing her scowl, he hastily added, "But Max and I will help if you need it, of course."

Rolling her eyes, Gina said, "Thanks Tad, but I think I've got this one."

Turning to Leonardo, she began. "This stuff is complicated. Doctors have to study for years before they can start to treat patients, so don't expect a 10-second medical education. Okay? A large number of diseases are caused by microbes. Some people call them germs, but that's not really a very helpful term. The easier way to remember is to understand that there are four basic types of microbes. These microbes are teeny-tiny organisms that enter the body and cause disease. You can't see a microbe unless you are using a microscope."

"Microscope?"

"Yes. It's a device with a glass that enlarges small things to make them look larger," said Gina. She knew her recital of her recent microbe lesson would take long enough without her stopping to be distracted by an explanation of a microscope, so she refused to go off on a tangent, even for Leonardo da Vinci. She pulled a bobby pin from her hair and continued. "The four basic types of microbes are viruses, bacteria, fungi, and protozoa. A virus is so small that millions of them could fit on the tip of this bobby pin."

Leonardo examined the pin and repeated, pointing to the top of the pin, "Millions of viruses can fit on this?"

"Yes. A virus enters into living cells, and once inside the cells, takes command and changes the mechanism that controls the function of that cell. In the process, the viruses reproduce by injecting nucleic acid—such as DNA—into the machinery of cells. The cell is often destroyed during this process. When that occurs, a person gets sick with what is known as a viral illness." Gina gestured wildly with her hands in an attempt to help Leonardo understand, but her extensive hand waving also told Tad and Max that she was getting pretty excited about the topic.

"The next type of microbe is bacteria," Gina continued. "Bacteria are usually single-celled organisms that are *much larger* than viruses. Humans can see them by looking through a microscope." She paused to consider for a moment before holding up one of her hands in a fist and said, "If a virus were the size of your fist, a bacterium would be the size of your entire body." She jumped out of her chair to illustrate the size of a human body.

Tad and Max exchanged amused looks. Even though they couldn't understand what she was saying, it was still pretty funny watching her get this excited.

Gina however, didn't notice their amusement and continued her explanation. "Bacteria also cause disease by killing cells, but they do it in a different way. Food, in the form of nutrients, flows through the body in the red blood cells, which are like the food delivery guys for all the parts of the body. When the red blood cells arrive with the food, the bacteria grab it first and release a poison that kills the cells. Each type of bacteria targets a particular part of the body, and that part of the body determines the type of disease the human will suffer."

"Not all bacteria are harmful, though. Some are friendly and have important and useful functions," said Dr. Kastleboro, interrupting Gina. "But that's a lesson for another day and another teacher." He smiled and nodded to Gina to continue.

Seeing Leonardo's look of consternation, Gina asked, "Do you understand what I'm talking about?"

"No," he admitted, smiling self-consciously, "but please continue. What I am able to understand is fascinating, and I need to learn it all if I am to succeed."

Gina nodded and continued her explanation. "Okay, so the thing that caused the Black Plague was a bacterium, and that is why modern medicine can cure it. Bacteria can be destroyed by medicines we call antibiotics, such as penicillin. Penicillin mimics the food the bacteria eat, so the bacteria gobble up the penicillin—which has no nutritional value—get stuffed, and then die because they really ate nothing substantial. Then the disease is cured!"

She said the last sentence so triumphantly that Tad and Max applauded. Gina sheepishly sat down in her chair again, but Leonardo was as absorbed in Gina's explanation as she was.

"The third type of microbe is protozoa," Gina said after taking a sip of her drink. "Many protozoa are the same size as bacteria, but unlike most bacteria that have hard outer shells, most protozoa instead have a soft outer casing. Protozoa can range in size from microscopic to really big, like flat tapeworms, which are disgusting. They can become as long as 20 feet. My cousin had one once and I ..." she trailed off for a moment, then shook her head and addressed the topic at hand. "Anyway, protozoa have many ways of causing disease, but they mostly do it by taking the nutrients from our cells.

"The fourth type of microbe is a fungus. These are microbes that grow into colonies, deploying thin tentacles that destroy human cells. There are some friendly bacteria in the body that sometimes will destroy fungi, and there's medicine that can help, too."

"How often do 'microbes' actually attack a person?" Leonardo asked.

Gina shook her head. "*Attack* is not entirely the right word. Microbes are everywhere. The average person confronts thousands of microbes every day."

"Then why are we not sick all day, every day?" Leonardo looked puzzled.

"Because of our immune system."

"What is that?"

For the first time, Gina felt like they had reached a topic she couldn't explain. "Well," she said slowly, "everybody has a system inside their body that fights against microbes."

"Let me field this question," interrupted Dr. Kastleboro. "Simply put, it works like this. We all have an immune system that protects us. It is truly a marvelous system. It is also the most complex of our bodily systems. The body, just like every living thing, is made up of cells. A cell is the smallest living organism that can survive on its own."

"I thought you said these microbes are living things," said Leonardo, confused. *It just doesn't add up*, he thought to himself. *Microbes are smaller than cells, and cells are the smallest things alive, but microbes are alive?*

"Well, yes," Dr. Kastleboro tried to explain. "Microbes are at least one cell in size, sometimes larger. But, because of the complexity of nature, that rule does not apply to viruses, which are not in the same category as bacteria. Viruses are not living things in the same sense."

Leonardo held up his hands to halt Dr. Kastleboro's explanation. "I'm sorry. I need to know more, much more, but I do not understand what you have just told me. Are people made up of cells?"

"Yes. People, as well as animals and plants—everything that lives is made of cells. Each cell is its own little factory, performing its own special tasks. Cells are very complex units that make up the basic structure of every human," Dr. Kastleboro clarified.

Gina summarized the conversation for Max and Tad, who had begun to feel left out.

"When we get back," Tad whispered to Max when Gina wasn't paying attention, "I'm going to have to start learning another language. I hate this whole translating thing. It makes conversations take *forever*." He knew that if Gina heard his comment, she would pester him about it once they got back home.

Before Max could respond, Leonardo said, "Gina just explained that when harmful microbes enter the body, they kill the cells of that body. If that is so, then how can it be that there are any humans still alive today?"

"That is what I am trying to explain, Maestro," said Dr. Kastleboro. "Inside of our bodies, invisible to us, we have a system that fights microbes and protects the cells. We call it the immune system, and it's mostly made up of white blood cells. Their job is to travel around in the body and destroy microbes."

"Then these are also cells in our bodies?" Leonardo asked carefully.

"Yes. There are numerous types of white blood cells. Some work on the front lines of attack, defeating microbes before they get very far. Some are helper cells, others are suppressor cells, and still others remove dead microbes to help keep the body in good form. Quite miraculously, they all work together. It is how we stay healthy most of the time."

Dr. Kastleboro was proud of how much he remembered on the immune system from when he was a student. Ms. Howder-shell would have done a better job, but she wasn't around to help out. However, he had reached the end of his immune system knowledge, and was relieved to see that Leonardo was looking a little overwhelmed. He could stop explaining.

After a moment, Leonardo shook his head and ran his hand over his mouth and beard. He sighed and dropped his hand into his lap. There was just so much he had to learn.

Then he remembered the department store and how there seemed to be captured sunlight hanging from the ceilings. "How is it that you contain sunlight indoors? I haven't seen candles, but you have found a way to somehow illuminate the indoors."

"That's with the help of electricity," Max explained.

"Please allow me to ask you about this thing you call electricity. It has been on my mind all day. Could someone explain it to me? And perhaps you could direct me to one of those units powered by this electricity force. I believe I could fashion one of those units of electricity to operate a machine I once designed for manned flight.

"It has always been my dream to use a machine to fly like the birds. It is my belief that with the right power, such a machine could be built. On his own, no man is strong enough for the sustained motion needed for flight. This electrical force may be just what I need. Then at last I could build a device in which a man could actually fly through the air." He was grinning as his hands twisted through the air, imitating his flying machine. Gina translated for Max and Tad.

"A flying machine would be a great invention for mankind, that's for sure," said Dr. Kastleboro. "But I'm sorry, Maestro. A flying machine was invented almost a hundred years ago, and today the world is filled with thousands, even millions, of them. We call them airplanes."

Leonardo frowned and shook his head. "Once again, too late," he muttered to himself. To the group, he said, "Well, then, where might I see such a machine?"

They looked at each other.

"I'm not sure that's going to be possible, at least not right now," said Dr. Kastleboro. "You see, you can only see an airplane up close at an airport. The closest airport is way out of the city, and we don't have a car." He paused. "But we'll see. Perhaps later."

"Boy, that would be fun," said Tad after Gina translated for him.

"Yes. Perhaps later," Dr. Kastleboro repeated.

The three friends looked at each other, knowing that when Dr. Kastleboro used the word *later*, he usually meant *never*.

7. THE PLAN

The regional tabloid, *La Nazione*, had editorial offices in a building with a glass storefront. Above were three stories of tall, vertical windows encased in a narrow framework, giving the appearance of a jailhouse. Inside, Antonio Gigliardi, from the local television station, met with Giuseppe Cecchi, editorial director, and Matteo Renaldi, the mayor of Florence.

"Okay, Antonio," said the mayor, a small man with a sharp chin underscoring a peninsula of a nose. "What is so important that I needed to rush over here?" He eased into the editor's swivel chair and leaned back.

Antonio jumped right in. "This afternoon, I saw a costumed man on a bicycle almost collide with a car."

"And …?"

"The guy on the bicycle was dressed like he belonged in the 16th century. When he was asked to identify himself, he claimed to be Leonardo da Vinci. He sounded so convincing it was almost scary."

"da Vinci?" Giuseppe and Mayor Renaldi both chuckled.

"He's a little past his prime, isn't he? I mean, a man can get pretty wrinkled in 500 years!" quipped the mayor.

"That's the point," said Antonio. "I didn't get a chance to find out who he really was since he wouldn't stop insisting that he was Leonardo da Vinci returned from the dead. Still, I got some great videos of the guy, and as an actor, he's good. And he does resemble pictures of the great Maestro. It's a bit uncanny, to be honest."

"Well," said the mayor, "If you're going to play Leonardo, this is the place to do it. So what's the idea?"

"Publicity, Mr. Mayor. Publicity," said Giuseppe, moving a stapler away from the side of a desk and propping himself on the edge.

"I'm not following you."

"Remember The Battle of Anghiari?" asked Antonio.

"The battle of what?"

"The famous painting that Leonardo da Vinci never finished," said Antonio. "In 1504, the counsel of Florence commissioned da Vinci to paint one wall in the Hall of Five Hundred with a scene from the *Battle of Anghiari*. His competitor, Michelangelo, was to paint a scene from the *Battle of Cascina* on the opposite wall. Leonardo signed a contract with the Signoria of Florence to make the painting, but he never finished it. He made a sketch, put down some paint, but then left Florence for Milan. He never completed his contract."

"I must be missing something here. At what point did you say how this stunt will give Florence publicity?" said the mayor.

Antonio began to walk around the room in excitement. "See, Mr. Mayor, he was paid city money, and then the Maestro breached his contract. The famous Leonardo da Vinci owes the city of Florence a painting. And we've already paid him for it!

"Now, Mayor Renaldi, it would make for a great news story if that guy pretending to be Leonardo da Vinci fulfilled the real Maestro's contract. The man owes Florence. He has to finish the painting of the *Battle of Anghiari*."

"But who cares?" said the mayor. "Who, today, even knows what the Battle of Anghiari was or what it was about?"

"That stuff's not important," said Antonio. "The memory of the painting was made famous by Peter Paul Rubens, who made his own painting of Leonardo's original work. The concept of the painting is famous because it is a dynamic presentation of horses and men locked in a mortal struggle.

"Just picture the scene. If he's a terrible artist, audiences will love it when he makes a fool of himself trying to paint like da Vinci—if he wants to keep insisting he's Leonardo da Vinci, he'll have to display his artistic talents. Most likely, he'll make some excuse. Doesn't matter. Picture the story: Leonardo da Vinci returns, but refuses to finish his painting. It will make great TV and newspaper copy. More importantly, Florence, for a few shining moments, will be featured by news outlets across the world. Right now, there are no major wars going on, and we don't even have a scandal. It's a slow news season. Everyone wants something interesting to follow in the news, and that's what we have here in Florence!" Antonio was now pounding a desk with enthusiasm.

The mayor thought it over seriously. After a few moments, he asked, "Okay, let's say I agree to go along with the plan. Where do we find this guy?"

Antonio and Giuseppe looked at each other and shrugged.

"Actually, right now," said Antonio, "I'm not sure. But we'll find him. A man in a Leonardo costume can't hide easily in this town. In fact, I'm already running a little piece about the car accident on the evening news."

"But," said the Mayor, "what if he really is Leonardo da Vinci, and what if he really does finish the painting? How much will the city owe him? And who is going to pay him?"

Both Antonio and Giuseppe burst into laughter. "Who cares?" they guffawed in unison.

Then, laughing even harder, Antonio said, "Maybe he'll take American Express!"

8. THE AIRPLANE

The next day, Leonardo rode shotgun in the taxi while Max, Gina, and Tad squeezed tightly together in the back seat. The taxi driver was taking them out of Florence along the Via del Ponte toward Peretola Airport. Leonardo was amazed that, even at the great speeds they were traveling, the vehicle could stop swiftly whenever the driver needed to slow down. Other similar vehicles, some bigger, some smaller, sped along the multilane, smooth, black roadway. The others in the taxi seemed to be relaxed, as if the speed were unremarkable, but da Vinci was clutching the canvas webbing that strapped him into the seat. He had never traveled faster than 25 kilometers per hour on the back of a galloping horse. Now, he was rolling along the black roadway going 100! He was amazed to see women driving these horseless carts, too, sometimes going even faster than the taxi.

"These machines are so big and heavy, how can women handle the controls?" he asked.

"Cosa?" asked the driver, a confused look on his face.

"With levers and hydraulics," said Gina quickly, understanding the question and trying to occupy her companion and prevent him from proclaiming himself the great Leonardo da Vinci again.

Leonardo looked confused, "but the complexity?"

"To tell you the truth, Maestro," said Gina, smiling, "it is quite easy for a woman to be more skilled than a man."

Leonardo was too caught up in watching the cars around them to even ask what she meant by the comment.

The taxi exited onto the Autostrade del Mare and then swung into the entrance to the terminal. Before them was the wide sweep of the single-story, combined arrival and departure entrance lined with glass doors, a concrete sidewalk, and a broad, overhanging canopy that stretched the length of the terminal. In front was a large parking area filled with cars.

Leonardo was fascinated. In his journey, he had not seen a single horse or ox—or any animals at all, except for an occasional dog and cat. *Had these machines completely replaced working animals?* He'd have to ask later.

The taxi turned away from the entrance onto a narrow, unpaved road and sped along the fence surrounding the open airfield. To their left stretched the 8,000 foot (2,438 meters) runway. Unlike larger airports, the Peretola had only a single runway.

As they passed beyond the terminal, three jet airplanes— two twin engine Boeing 757s and one twin engine Airbus A300—were parked at the back of the terminal.

"What form of buildings are those?" asked Leonardo, pointing to the three jet airliners. He was amazed at the size and streamlined design of what appeared to be sleek, giant buildings with rows of windows.

"They're not buildings," answered Gina. "They're airplanes. Jet airplanes."

"What do they do?"

"Why, they carry passengers. People use them to travel in the air to other cities or countries."

"They fly? But they are so massive," was all that Leonardo could think to say. *This new world is much more than I had imagined. Who could have imagined, back then, how much the world would change? We had no idea how many limitations we faced. I certainly had no idea how they restricted even my remarkable vision. I need to learn more.*

"But the airplane we're renting won't be anywhere close to the size of those jets," Gina added.

Leonardo listened, but did not understand.

On the far side of the airfield was a small hangar with five miniature airplanes parked beside it. The man who would be their pilot was fueling one of the planes. He waved to them as the taxi pulled up to the front of the hangar. They all got out of the taxi, and Gina turned to Tad, who was carrying most of the spending cash they had for this trip. They had been able to come up with just enough money to pay for the plane and taxi. Tad gave some lire to Gina and she paid the driver.

As the taxi departed, the pilot finished refueling and approached them. *"L'aereo è pronto,"* he said in Italian, placing his hand on his plane, "but I can't take all of you, only three passengers."

The pilot was a thin, lanky man who seemed to have more knees and elbows than he needed. His eyes were hidden behind dark sunglasses, and his sandy brown hair was captured beneath a dirty, well-worn baseball cap.

Gina replied to the pilot, saying, "No problem." Neither Max nor Tad understood what was being said.

She continued in Italian, "I'll wait and watch from here while the boys enjoy the ride." Gina would have really liked to go, but there was only room for two more passengers with the pilot and Maestro. She had taken a small plane ride last summer when her family toured the Grand Canyon. She knew that neither Tad or Max had ever been in a small plane before.

"Suits me," said the pilot.

The airplane was an American-made, top-winged Cessna 172 Skyhawk. It was gleaming white with bright red stripes and a red tail and rudder. Gina thought it looked like an enormous tube of Colgate toothpaste with wings. Max and Tad saw it as a great new adventure.

That morning, they had snuck out of the hotel to meet Leonardo by the statue of David. They knew that none of their teachers would have ever approved of the private plane ride, and if they found out, the trio would most certainly be in trouble. But Max, Tad, and Gina figured that as long as no one knew, they would be fine.

Leonardo understood that it had to be a secret, and though he did not like the idea of getting the teenagers in trouble, his concern for their welfare was far outweighed by his excitement. That morning, Leonardo da Vinci's dream from five centuries ago would become a reality. He would fly.

"Is this the airplane we will use to fly?" asked Leonardo.

The pilot overheard the question. *"Ciao. Sono Carlino,"* he introduced himself. Then, continuing in Italian, "This is a solid machine. I think it is one of the best. The original Cessna 170 was a tail-dragger, a real workhorse, but when they upgraded to the tricycle gear, they made it much better. This one is a dream machine."

They walked to the airplane and the three students looked inside.

"Oh, man," said Tad. "I've never been this close to a plane like this."

"Me neither," said Max.

They ran their hands over the smooth surface and looked into the cockpit. The inside had the faint odor of engine oil, hydraulic fluid, and gasoline.

"Wow," said Tad. "They don't make perfume that smells this good."

"There's a reason for that," said Gina, pulling a face.

The boys did not respond. They were too fascinated with the instrument panel: altimeter, turn-and-bank, directional-gyro, air speed indicator, fuel gauge, oil pressure gauge, and magnetic compass.

Meanwhile, Leonardo followed closely behind the pilot as he did his preflight inspection, testing the flex and movement of the ailerons, rudder, and elevator.

After they completely circled the plane, Leonardo said, "I don't see a mechanism to twist and flap the wings."

The pilot cocked his head, wondering about his passenger. There was something familiar about this blond-haired, bearded man, but he couldn't put his finger on it. Still, he was a paying passenger, and that counted for a lot. He explained, "Birds may flap their wings to fly, but airplanes don't need to. The reason birds flap their wings is to get forward thrust like a swimmer using his arms in order to gain thrust in the water. On an airplane, the propeller gives the thrust needed by spinning. I'm sure you've felt the force of moving air in wind storms when you walk against the flow. When you do that, you're producing drag. The thrust of the airplane overcomes the drag caused by the resistance of the friction of the airplane itself.

"We build airplanes with streamlined designs, like the wheel covers on this one, in order to reduce friction, or, in other words, to reduce drag. The less drag, the less power we need for the propeller to pull the airplane through the air."

Leonardo listened carefully to the explanation as the pilot rattled on in Italian. He didn't understand all the words, but didn't want to interrupt.

The pilot continued, "Now, the third force involved in flight is the weight of the airplane. That is the force of gravity pulling the airplane down. In order to make the airplane fly, to overcome gravity, we have the wings. But not flapping wings—they've been tried in the past and they don't work. Wrong theory. It is the wings being pulled through the air by the thrust of the propeller that allows the airplane to fly."

"What is it about the wings that makes that possible?" asked Gina, guessing the question that must have been on Leonardo's mind.

"It's the shape. It gives the airplane its principal lift. Every wing must be the correct size to lift the weight of the plane, given the speed at which the airplane will be pulled through the air.

"However, the most important thing is how the wings are built." Running his hand along the front of the wing of the Cessna, Carlino continued, "You can see that the wing is curved on the top and straight on the bottom. When the airplane is pulled through the air by the propeller, the air particles separate and pass over the top of the wing and along the underside. The separated air particles arrive at the rear of the wing at the same time. The air over the curved top travels faster than the air along the flat bottom. As a result, the air traveling over the top is thinner than the air along the bottom. The faster air, being thinner, has less pressure than the slower, thicker air along the bottom. The airplane flies because the wing lifts from the greater air pressure under the wings to the lesser air pressure above the wings. It's called Bernoulli's Principle."

He demonstrated by waving his flat hand in an arc. Leonardo watched closely, doing his best to piece it all together with his own understanding of flight.

The pilot, seeing that the passengers were genuinely interested, continued. "A lot of the earlier attempts to build flying machines failed because the wings were simply large kites and did not apply this important principle. I've seen sketches done by Leonardo da Vinci in which he tried to design a flying machine with flapping wings. Even if he had really built it, it wouldn't have worked."

Leonardo was glad he had not introduced himself, because he hadn't thought of the air pressure principle. As hard as he had tried, he had not figured out what now seemed so obvious.

"*Va bene,*" announced the pilot. "Enough ground school. Let's get flying!"

The two boys clambered into the back seats and strapped themselves in. Then Leonardo climbed into the passenger seat and fumbled around, trying to figure out the safety belt. The pilot got into the left front seat, reached over to help Leonardo with the straps, and then strapped himself in.

The pilot's hands moved quickly over the control panel, snapping switches before he finally pulled the starter, causing the airplane to roar to life. He revved the engine, watched the oil pressure climb, verified that his gas tanks were full, checked the mags, and released the brakes. The airplane began to move.

As they rolled along the designated taxiway toward the runway, they paused as an Airbus moved ahead for a takeoff position. The large jet towered above them, its twin engines screaming with enormous power.

For the teenage boys, a week of old buildings and old history paled in comparison to a secret flight in a Cessna. This was more like it. Tad was glad that Gina had devised the plan for them to meet up with Leonardo and go flying. How great that she was able to work with the hotel concierge to make the arrangements.

"I'm sure glad you could do this," Tad had confided to Gina earlier. "I've never heard of a concierge. I thought it was just a fancy Italian word you knew."

Leonardo stared at the giant jet plane slowly gliding in front of them. It was close enough to them that he could see people looking out the long row of windows. Its size was overwhelming. He still wondered if it was possible for such a large machine to actually lift into the air.

The jet motored to the end of the taxiway and swung smoothly onto the runway. With a mighty roar that overpowered all other sounds and shook their waiting Cessna, the Airbus began to roll, picking up speed quickly. By the time it was two-thirds of the way down the runway, it lifted into the air, swallowed the landing gear into its belly, and climbed steeply away.

Leonardo was speechless.

"Now it's our turn," said the pilot. He pressed the throttle and the plane rolled onto the runway. Before them was the wide expanse of white concrete. The pilot held the brakes and increased the power by pushing the throttle to the full open position. The engine roared. He then released the brakes, and the Cessna gave a slight leap. Leonardo clutched the sides of his seat while the small airplane accelerated at an ever-increasing speed down the broad sea of concrete. He did not know what to expect as they sped down the runway. They did not notice the plane pulling slightly toward the left while the pilot applied an even pressure with his right foot on the right rudder pedal to overcome the natural torque from the pull of the spinning propeller.

The airplane quickly reached flying speed, and its wheels lifted from the runway. The plane was in the air, and there was a sudden smoothness. It appeared to rise effortlessly, the ground dropping away. As they ascended, the view of the green rolling hills of Tuscany began to expand before them, making them feel like they were slowing down. Of course, they weren't. It was just that the normal reference points to give the sense of speed were moving away as they climbed through the crisp morning air. Below them, houses, plowed fields, vineyards and lines of tall Cypress trees looked like a museum exhibit.

"Non lo avrei mai sognato!" exclaimed Leonardo as he stared in awe at the panorama spreading before them. This really was beyond his wildest dreams. As the airplane climbed further upward, all of Florence appeared like a three-dimensional relief map of the city.

"Wow," was the only word either of the boys could muster. They had, of course, flown into Florence on a big jet, but looking out the small window of a commercial jetliner could not compare to the sweeping panorama viewed from this Cessna.

"How do you control the airplane?" asked Leonardo.

"It's controlled mostly with the yoke," the pilot answered, inclining his head toward the steering wheel shaped like the top half of an H. "I'm steering with it. If you watch the yoke in front of your position, you can see that when I want to turn, I turn the yoke slightly like a steering wheel and hold back a little to keep the airplane flying level, or, in the present case, climbing smoothly. To make the turn smooth and to keep us comfortable in our seats, I pull back with firm, but gentle, pressure on the yoke. I apply a little pressure to the pedal on the floor for whichever way I'm turning—left pedal for a left turn, right pedal for a right one. The pedals control the large rudder at the tail of the airplane. As long as I hold pressure on the yoke, I am directing the airplane to keep climbing. When I want to stop climbing and fly level, I simply release the pressure. No heavy moves, just gentle, firm pressure."

Slowly, the scene below grew broader. The cars, the houses, and the buildings became distant. When they reached 5,000 feet (1,524 meters), the pilot leveled their flight and began a circling tour of the region.

"This truly is far beyond any dream I ever imagined," gasped Leonardo.

"Why?" asked the pilot. "Did you dream of becoming a pilot?"

"I dreamed of inventing a flying machine," Leonardo said, forgetting his previous embarrassment about not knowing how integral air pressure was for the lift necessary to allow an airplane to fly.

"Yeah, I guess a lot of people did, but the Wright Brothers got there first," the pilot laughed.

For a while, they flew in silence, each in their own thoughts. Finally, the pilot said to Leonardo, "Would you like to get a feel for the controls?"

"Si, Si!"

"Just put both of your hands on the yoke in front of you. Don't let your feet touch the pedals. I'll handle them."

Leonardo followed his instruction.

"Now follow me as I turn the airplane." The pilot began a slow left turn, banking slightly, holding back pressure to keep the airplane flying level. Leonardo followed through with a jerking touch. "Not so rough," said the pilot. "To climb, just pull back slightly on the yoke."

It was at that moment that all went wrong. Without calculating his own strength or the sensitivity of the controls, Leonardo yanked the yoke back toward his chest. The nose of the airplane rose abruptly and, surprised, Leonardo stomped his foot on the left rudder pedal.

"No! per carità!" yelled the pilot, eyes wide.

The nose of the airplane was yanked straight up. The engine strained and the airplane felt as if it were falling backward, stalling. In an instant, the airplane flipped over toward the left and went on its back, falling into a left-spiraling tailspin.

"Attento!" shouted the pilot again, grabbing at the yoke.

"Whoa!" screamed Max. Leaning forward from the back seat, Max and Tad were suddenly looking straight down at the Earth below. Farms and fields and houses and roads spun beneath them like something out of the *Wizard of Oz*.

Sensing their plunge toward the earth below, Leonardo pulled back hard on the yoke.

"No, no, lascialo!" the pilot shouted as he tried to wrest the yoke from Leonardo. *"Mollalo, lascialo andare, cretino.* We're in a tailspin! We're in a stall with no airflow over the wings. Let go! I have to pop the yoke to break the stall!" His words flowed out so fast they were hard to understand. Of course, neither Max nor Tad could understand the Italian anyway, but they could see the pilot struggling with Leonardo.

"I am strong. I can pull us up from the fall," said Leonardo with a calmness that revealed his lack of understanding of their immediate and mortal danger. He held the yoke in a white-knuckled, powerful grip.

"*Lo devi lasci aree!*" screamed the pilot, struggling to tug Leonardo's fingers off of the yoke. "You're going to kill us all!"

A million thoughts went through Max's head. He stared in fear at the earth spinning below, growing ever closer as they hurtled downward. He had the strange thought that if they were killed in an airplane crash, the teachers, his mother, and his father would all be upset—no, furious—that he and Tad had put themselves in this danger with a man who had already been dead once before. He felt bad that poor Gina would probably blame herself because she had arranged this flight. But then, these were silly thoughts. He was just plain scared of dying.

Tad was not as contemplative as Max, and he was never much for planning. He knew that action was needed… now! Quickly, he unfastened his seat belt, leaned forward, and mustering all of his strength, slapped both of Leonardo's ears hard with his open hands. Leonardo was stunned. The shock of the blow against his ears caused him to momentarily release the yoke. This was just enough time for the pilot to grab his own yoke, pop it forward out of Leonardo's grip, and press it to the control panel.

At the same moment, he pressed the right rudder pedal. The spinning stopped and the airplane lurched forward. They could feel the lift from the air flowing once again over the wings. Now they were flying, but in a nose dive. The airplane began to pick up speed. Firmly, but smoothly, the pilot pulled back on the yoke. Gravity pulled them down into their seats as they pulled G's like fighter pilots in combat. The pilot was firm at the controls, but cautious not to overstress the wings, as that might cause them to collapse.

Almost in slow motion, the plane began to lift as they raced toward a stand of slim, stately Cypress trees. The pilot held the Cessna level, heading straight toward the trees as he allow-ed the air speed to build. At the last moment, he pulled back

on the yoke, holding it steady against his stomach. Leonardo
reached up to his yoke to assist, but the pilot slapped his hands.
The plane began to pull more G's again, driving them all down
into their seats as the Cessna barely lifted over the trees—
coming close enough to frighten a handful of birds who were
not expecting to be attacked by an airplane.

"Great work, kid," said the pilot in English, nodding toward Tad.

Then he turned to Leonardo and shouted, "*Lei signore e' un cretino!* You nearly killed us all! Do not touch the controls or pedals again!"

"Well, I—"

"And never ever fight with the pilot of a plane. Ever!"

No one spoke while the pilot eased the airplane back up to 5,000 feet (1,524 meters) and returned to level flight. "We'll head west toward Pisa, take an aerial look at the leaning tower, then go back home," the pilot said, now speaking calmly as if nothing happened.

"*Sono davvero spiacente,*" said Leonardo, softly. "Truly sorry."

"I'm sure you are," the pilot said flatly. Then he paused and said, "Anyway, during our little exciting adventure, I suddenly remembered why you look familiar. You're the guy who was all over the newspaper this morning."

"The what?"

Now the pilot grinned. "Big headline in *La Nazione* with a full color picture of you lying flat out on the hood of a car dressed in some kind of costume. The headline was something like *Leonardo da Vinci returns to Florence: 16th century costumed man causes a stir!* I didn't recognize you out of costume, but you're the guy who claims to be returned from the dead. You do favor the pictures I've seen of Leonardo. What are you, some kind of actor?"

"No, I *am* Leonardo da Vinci."

"Ha! You came very close to being the *late* Leonardo da Vinci... again!" the pilot said.

The pilot pointed forward, where the outline of the leaning tower of Pisa began to appear. He dropped to a lower altitude and made several circles around the famous tower. Meanwhile, he seemed to be spending time on his radio conferring with the Peretola Tower. On the return, he flew them over Siena and circled over Florence where the remains of the old walls and fortifications could easily be seen from the air.

"I gather that walled cities are no longer necessary," said Leonardo dully.

"All one country," the pilot replied, momentarily pausing his radio call.

As they approached the airport, Max and Tad could make out cars, TV trucks, and a mob of people milling around the small hangar.

"Oh, no," said Max, tapping the pilot on the shoulder and pointing down. The pilot smiled and nodded.

Leonardo followed their gestures. "What are all those people doing?"

"That's your welcoming committee, Mr. da Vinci. After I recognized you, I realized that if I called some of my friends at *La Nazione* and told them that I was being honored by none other than Leonardo da Vinci, I could probably get a little publicity for my flight business. I'm sure you won't mind helping me out, considering that stunt you pulled back there."

Neither Max nor Tad could understand what the two were saying, but looking down at the gathering crowd, Max said to Tad, "I think the Maestro has more trouble."

The pilot continued to speak to Leonardo. "But I'll tell you, my radio call was as strange as you are. Whoever answered at the newspaper said they already knew you were flying with me. I don't know how that could be."

What the pilot didn't know was there was one person willing to out Leonardo in order to embarrass his classmates. His name was Neville Klaxton. When Neville woke up that morning, he realized that Tad, Gina and Max weren't anywhere to be seen. Hoping to catch them doing something wrong, he went down to the first floor and surveyed the lobby. Then he thought of the concierge. He knew that if they were planning an adventure in this strange city, Gina, who had lived in Italy, would know enough to seek help from this hotel serviceman.

He approached the concierge's desk. "Excuse me, my good man," he said, trying to appear worldly.

The concierge resisted a smile and responded politely. "*Sì, Signore?* How may I be of assistance?"

"My three friends?"

"Ah, yes—a redheaded girl, a tall boy, and another boy who was wearing glasses?"

"Yes. Did they say anything to you about what they were doing today? A museum, perhaps?"

"Why, yes, they did. They had me reserve an airplane at Peretola and a cab to take them there. But that was much earlier. It's not likely you will be able to catch up with them now."

"No problem," said Neville. He pretended to walk away, but then turned sharply back to the concierge. "Oh, by the way, do you know the phone number of the *La Nazione* newspaper?"

"Of course," said the concierge. "Just pick up that phone by the table and I'll dial it for you." In a few minutes, Neville conveyed Leonardo da Vinci's location to a reporter at the paper. "Let's see how you guys handle this," he said to no one in particular.

Back at the airfield, the pilot turned for his final approach and guided the Cessna to a gentle, floating landing as the wheels touched softly onto the runway. The turned at the first taxiway and rolled to a stop beside the hangar. As soon as the engine died and the propeller stopped spinning, the waiting crowd pressed around the Cessna.

As Leonardo stepped from the airplane cabin, the mayor of Florence rushed toward him with his hand outstretched. "Welcome home to Florence, Mr. da Vinci! It's been a long time, but you're still quite famous."

9. THE NEW CHALLENGE

Max and Tad eased themselves out of the airplane. As people reached out to shake Leonardo's hand, Antonio Gigliardi held them back to allow his cameraman good shots of the event. Meanwhile, two reporters from the paper were firing questions too fast for Leonardo to answer. Neither Max nor Tad could understand what was being said. They searched for Gina.

"I understand that by some miracle, you have been restored to life in the 21st century," said the mayor. "Since you are still very much a hero in Florence, we have arranged a greeting at the Uffizi."

Leonardo was pleased. As nice as the American teacher and his students had been, he realized that he needed to discuss his quest with those with a higher education, hopefully professors at a university. This remarkable greeting and recognition was a blessing.

"I shall be delighted," Leonardo replied with a smile. "I am hopeful that you will be able to help me with my quest."

"Your *quest*?" the mayor asked, confused.

"Yes. I need to use my intellectual gifts to discover or invent something for the betterment of all mankind."

"A noble quest, eh?" Gigliardi started to chuckle, but then thought better of it. He nodded, "Yes, something worthy of such a man as yourself."

Slowly, Gina worked her way through the swarm of people, trying to find Max and Tad. Leonardo was in the midst of the crowd, and the pilot was also doing his share of answering reporters' questions, but with so many people around, it was hard to locate the other passengers from the short plane ride. Gina was puzzled by the events, but, picking up tidbits of the conversation, she began to understand what was going on. When she finally found Tad and Max, they were anxious to know what was going on.

"Somehow, the press learned that the Maestro was in that airplane," she said, "They're all talking about Leonardo's return to new life and having some type of celebration back in Florence."

"Are they serious?" asked Max.

"I can't say for sure," said Gina, "but I don't think so."

"Then why all the fuss?" asked Tad.

"That's just the point," said Gina. "I don't get it."

As they talked amongst themselves, the mayor led Leonardo through the crowd to a shiny black Maserati. The driver held the door open for the two men to climb in. Leonardo was so excited about being given an honored greeting, he forgot about Gina, Max, and Tad.

When they saw that he was about to be whisked away, the teenagers furiously elbowed their way through the crowd, trying to catch him.

"*Maestro, aspetta!*" shouted Gina.

Hearing Gina's voice, Leonardo stopped and turned back toward the airfield. He couldn't see them because of the jam of people around him.

"*Maestro, aspetta!*" Gina and Tad shouted together, with Tad imitating her Italian.

But they were too late. The mayor, hearing their voices, placed his hand on Leonardo's arm. "Hurry, *Signore, da Vinci.*

We must leave at once!" The mayor ushered him into the back seat, climbed in behind him, closed the door, and ordered the driver to depart.

As they drove out along the airport fence, the TV trucks followed. The rest of the crowd rushed into their cars and joined the caravan. Within minutes, the field was empty.

"Hey," yelled Tad. "Wait!" Then he shouted even louder, but to no avail. "Don't forget us!"

In the sudden calm, Max and Tad looked at Gina. Furious, she stammered, "How could he just go off and leave us? We brought him here!"

"This was his chance," said Max trying to calm her.

"He had an opportunity to get official help from important people."

Tad, too, tried to find a way to make sense of what just happened. "He wanted to meet people who could help him with his quest. If we're in this to help him, I guess we shouldn't blame him for wanting to connect with important people," Tad said, watching the cars drive away while taking a deep breath to calm down.

"Are we sure that's what it was?" Gina demanded. "I mean, are we sure he really is Leonardo da Vinci? We never really had time to sit down and discuss it. Maybe the teachers are right and he's nothing more than just a really good actor."

"But the gold florins!" Tad said emphatically. "*Those* were real."

Gina, who had been biting her bottom lip and thinking hard, spoke up. "I think you are right, Tad. If we were good science students," she smiled, "which we are, then we should apply the scientific process, as taught by Ms. Howdershell. We need more data."

Max nodded and pulled out his notebook. They all huddled around so they could see it as Max started a list. He wrote, "Hypothesis: The man is the real Leonardo da Vinci." Then he looked up at Tad and Gina and asked, "Okay, what data do we have? And I don't think the fact that he says he is counts as good data."

"The drawings of the horses' heads and writing backwards," offered Tad.

"There are those gold florins," repeated Gina. "Where else could he have gotten so many in such perfect condition?"

Max wrote it down and looked at Gina again.

"He sure knows a lot of stuff," she offered. "It would take a lifetime of research to know everything he knows without having to look it up every time. He never had any warning about what we were going to ask and he always had the perfect answer for events of olden times."

Max added "knowledge" to the list and then wrote "curiosity" beneath it. Looking up, he explained, "He consistently acted like he didn't know *anything* modern, and he was always asking questions. I don't think someone modern would think to ask questions about half the stuff he asked questions about."

"Is there anything else?" Gina asked, looking at Tad and Max questioningly.

They thought for a moment, and then Tad said, "How about how no one seems to know where he came from? There wasn't a single person who looked like they recognized him, and he just showed up in the piazza out of the blue."

"Good point, Tad," said Max, adding "out of the blue" to the list. Tad and Gina nodded and then all three stared at the list.

"I think that's all of it," said Gina. "Is there anything that proves our hypothesis to be wrong?"

"I don't know of anyone who has come back from the dead," said Tad, "that's a big, big piece of data against our hypothesis." He paused, rubbed his chin, smiled and added, "And all of our teachers insist that he is not really Leonardo da Vinci returned from the dead."

"Yes," added Gina, "Could teachers be wrong?"

"Yes," said Max. "The teachers don't believe he is real. That's good evidence that he is real." He laughed. "Therefore, our hypothesis must be true."

They all laughed.

Max wrote the words "Hypothesis Confirmed" at the bottom of the page and closed his notebook with a sigh. "I guess he really is the great Leonardo da Vinci then."

"But does our saying it really make it so?" conjectured Tad.

"Probably not," said Gina, "but I think he is who he says he is."

There was a pause, then Tad said, "Since he ditched us at the airport, I'm guessing that being legendary doesn't automatically make someone considerate."

Gina glumly nodded in agreement. "Either way, we are all real, and we have no way to get back to Florence."

"Now what?" asked Max.

"We can always walk to the terminal and find a taxi," said Gina, forgetting that they spent all of their money on the airplane ride.

"No, wait," said Tad, looking around the field. Turning toward the office near where the small planes parked, he pointed to an automobile with its hood up and steam pouring from the engine. "See that steam? That's our opportunity."

They all looked. A small, gray-haired man, stooped and angular, was leaning on a cane and peering helplessly into the malfunctioning engine.

"Follow me," said Tad as the three walked briskly toward the ailing automobile.

"Excuse me, sir," said Tad, forgetting that he needed Gina to translate. "It looks like you're having engine trouble."

The old man turned toward Tad's voice. "Ah, young man," he responded in broken English with a thick Italian accent. "Is that you speaking English, American English?"

"Yes, sir," said Tad, relieved that he could actually have a conversation without needing a translator.

"Ah," said the old man. "If you're American, then cars you know. Yes?"

"Oh, yes, sir. I know about cars."

"Well, good," said the man. "There is smoke in my car."

Tad and Max approached the car and looked into the engine cavity. "Steam," said Max, as if he had some idea of what was wrong with the car.

"Sure," said Tad, "but look." He pointed to a radiator hose that had come loose and was hanging down beside the engine block. "I don't think this beat-up old Fiat will run without the water pipes connected." He turned to the old man. "Pure science. Sir, I believe I can fix your car. In return, I wonder if you'd be so kind as to give my friends and me a ride back into Florence."

"Certainly," the man agreed. "If you don't mind my asking, what are you doing at the airport without any luggage?"

"We came with Leonardo da Vinci," Gina explained. "When he was offered a ride with the mayor, we were left behind."

"Ah," said the man. "Leonardo da Vinci. Yes. That's who I came here to see. On the television, I saw the story of him flying onto that car."

"A Citroën," said Tad.

"Well, yes. When I heard the mayor was coming to the airport to meet him, I thought it would be fun to see for myself this impressive imposter. But just as I arrived, my car burst into smoke and I seem to have missed the show."

Gina responded, "We've spent time with him. He's very nice, and we don't think he's an imposter."

"If he were nice, he wouldn't have left you here at the airport. And besides, from what little I saw of him, he didn't seem to be five hundred years old." The old man chuckled at his joke.

Meanwhile, Tad was peering into the engine. Pointing to the disconnected water hose, he said, "You just popped a water hose off the radiator. That happens with these older cars."

"So, what can we do with the popped hose?"

"Fix it," said Tad. "If I can borrow a screwdriver from that airplane hangar and a bucket of water, I'll have your car running in no time." He turned toward the hangar and started off at a trot to secure the tool and the water.

"Why did you want to see Leonardo da Vinci if you think he's just an imposter?" asked Gina.

"Real or fake, Leonardo da Vinci is the hero of our city. Allow me to formally introduce myself. I am Professor Ludwig Montebello, half German, half Italian, very old and very wise. As a professor of science and history at the *Universita degli Studi di Firenze*, I am a leading authority on that man. I have so many wonderful questions to ask him. If he is truly a genuine, other-worldly reincarnation, which I believe cannot be true, then I have much to ask." He waved his cane in the air. "If he is a fake, he will not know the answers to my questions; however, assuming he is an actor with Renaissance knowledge, I will have the pleasurable enjoyment of conversation."

Tad returned with the needed screwdriver and bucket of water. Leaning into the open motor, holding a wet rag in his hand to protect himself from the hot engine, he unscrewed the hose clamp, slipped it back on the radiator nozzle, clamped it back down, and then emptied the bucket of water into the yawning radiator top.

"There," said Tad. "Good as new."

"That is most marvelous," said the professor, bowing to Tad. "How can I thank you?"

Gina chimed in, "The ride into Florence is all we need."

"Not enough of a reward," answered Professor Montebello. "But it is a start."

As they approached the car, the professor said, "I must make one stop on the way. A small side trip to the Cirolo Golf Ugolina. A golf cart is to be loaned to me for this coming weekend for a festival at the university. They're even offering me their golf cart truck for ease of transportation. Very nice for me."

Max asked, "How come?"

"You mean the cart or why is it nice?" The professor hobbled to the car then struggled to fit his body into the driver's seat. He motioned the three into the car. Max and Gina climbed into the back seat while Tad rode in front.

"The cart," continued the professor, "I will need for the celebration. It's nice because I passed the golf course owner's son in history, a required course, though he should have failed."

When they were all strapped into the car, the professor hit the gas pedal with a thump of his foot. They roared across the field and along the wire fence. When they reached the gate, the professor made a sweeping, sliding, 90-degree turn onto the road, then drove through the main gate onto the highway.

Tad clutched the dashboard for balance, fighting through a wave of nausea. "Whew," he said, after it passed. His stomach hadn't fully recovered from the scare on the plane.

"Tell me," said the professor, "what exactly are you doing with Leonardo da Vinci? And why are you his friends?"

Gina explained Leonardo's quest. "No one else really believes he has come back to life, but we do. We want to help him do something great and live a long life... again!"

"Well," said the professor, "he should be glad for such loyalty and concern." At that moment, the car began to drift toward the center line of the highway.

"Hey!" shouted Tad as a large manure truck bore down on them from the opposite direction.

The professor looked up from his momentary lapse of attention to his driving just in time to jerk the automobile back onto the right side of the highway. "My, my," he said and continued racing along the highway.

"Professor, you seem to be sleepy," said Tad.

The professor nodded, then turned to Tad, "Would you be so kind as to drive?"

"No, no!" exclaimed Tad. "I know how, but I'm not old enough to hold a license. I could be in big trouble."

"Then not to worry."

They did not understand what he said or meant, but they all watched the professor carefully as he turned onto a private road and drove up to an ornate golf clubhouse. Clambering gratefully from the car, they climbed the steps and entered the large, elaborately decorated entrance hall. Immediately, a man with a round, owl-like head capped with thick, carrot-red hair, poked his face out of an office.

"*Il professor Montebello!*" exclaimed the man, rushing to greet the professor with a bear-like, manly hug. "*Bello vederti!*"

"It is good to see you, too! When may I expect to see you return to retake your history course?" teased the professor.

The red-headed man chuckled. "Never. Never, Professor. You might flunk me next time. Then dad would disinherit me."

"Then, young man, you owe me a golf cart."

The two men laughed and gave each other another enthusiastic hug.

"It's loaded and waiting, you wonderful old goat," said the younger man.

"Good. I'd like to stay and visit, but I'm behind schedule."

"That's okay. We'll talk when you get back." He retreated to his office and returned with a set of keys. "Here," he said, "the truck's out in the back."

Professor Montebello took charge of the truck and drove them into the old city of Florence. He drove erratically. Fortunately, all other drivers steered clear of the large, wandering vehicle.

As they drove, Gina said, "Professor, I have an idea."

"What would that be?"

"I think that the mayor took the Maestro into the city in order to either show him off or expose him as a fake. It doesn't matter which. Whatever his plan is, it will interfere with his quest."

"And your idea?"

"Once in the heart of the city, if you would let us use your golf cart, we will find him and bring him to you at your university. I think you could help him more than we can."

"Oh, yes, a private audience. But why will he go with you?"

"I think he trusts us. We helped him before."

"A private meeting with this man who pretends to be a ghost is an idea I like," said the professor.

When they reached Santa Maria Novella, the main railway station, he pulled the truck into a large parking area. Cars and taxis dropped off and picked up passengers. On the far side of the building was a busy bus depot. Everyone was intent on their own travel affairs, and paid no attention to the unloading of the golf cart. When the cart was on the street, Tad took control, Gina climbed in the front seat beside him, while Max scrambled into the back. Their next task was to locate Leonardo.

"Ah," said Professor Montebello. "If the mayor wants a spectacle, it is to the major piazza, most likely the Piazza della Signoria, there he will take him. That's always the place for public activity."

"Then that's where we should go," said Max.

The professor leaned toward the three students and whispered conspiratorially, "If you can get him into the cart, drive across the piazza to the Via del Calzaiuoli. This street will lead you right in front of the Duomo. Take a right turn around the Duomo then onto the Via Ricasoli, which in a few blocks will take you straight to the Piazza Di San Marco, a beautiful, tree-filled park directly in front of the university. You can't miss it. I am in the three-story, salmon, stucco building. Just enter the arched front door and follow the room designations."

Max made a careful note.

"Now," said the professor, pointing to the large, gray-stone church across the street from the railroad station. "That is the Santa Maria Novella. The best route to the Piazza della Signoria is to cross the street here and go past the church and turn right on Via Del Fossi. That street will take you straight toward the Arno River and the Ponte Vecchio. You'll recognize it—it is the famous bridge that has jewelry stores on the bridge itself. It will be jammed with tourists."

"That's just a few blocks from our hotel," said Max.

"Good," said the professor, "because just a few blocks down and to the left is the piazza. Be sure to turn left on one of the streets before you reach the river, then you will zig-zag a few streets to reach the piazza." The professor paused and considered his question. "When you get there, are you sure the Leonardo da Vinci person will go with you?"

"Pretty sure," said Gina. "As I explained, he trusts us."

"Besides," added Max, "if we tell him that we'll take him to a university to see a microscope, he won't be able to resist."

10. THE ENTERTAINER

Meanwhile, Dr. Kastleboro and Ms. Willoughby were in the Piazza della Signoria in search of their students.

"I thought they were just sleeping in," said Dr. Kastleboro, a worried look on his face, "but when I checked their rooms, they were gone."

Ms. Willoughby placed her hand over her mouth. She was also very concerned.

"Do you think they're all right?" asked Dr. Kastleboro. "Maybe we shouldn't have trusted them around that Leonardo actor. Maybe I shouldn't have been so friendly or bought him clothes."

"I think that maybe you—we—got caught up with the gold florins."

"I guess I wasn't thinking like a teacher—I should have."

"Well, none of the other kids seem to know where they went," said Ms. Willoughby. "Only Neville said he thought they were flying around Florence with the actor. I asked him if he meant sightseeing. He just shrugged his shoulders." She shook her head slowly. "But then he tried to hide a smirk, so I guess he was teasing and enjoying the fact that they were not around."

"What do you mean?"

"Oh, I don't know. The boys compete with each other. Part of the mystery of teenagers."

Dr. Kastleboro nodded, and trying to sound confident, declared, "I'm sure they're fine. I'd be really concerned if just one of them were missing. I'm sure they're fine," he repeated, as much to himself as to Ms. Willoughby. He added, "They're probably just wandering around looking at the vendors."

The two teachers walked toward the Duomo, looking carefully at the crowds gathered around the vendors, and checking down narrow streets where vendors opened their tents to reveal their wares.

The three students were nowhere to be seen.

Soon, they found their way into the Piazza della Signoria.

"These kids never think to ask for permission before they go off somewhere on their own," grumbled Dr. Kastleboro, frowning as he spoke.

It was now late morning, and several hours had passed since they discovered Max, Tad, and Gina's absence. Ms. Howdershell was keeping an eye on the other students while Dr. Kastleboro and Ms. Willoughby searched everywhere they could think to look. They were sure that the Leonardo da Vinci actor was with them—adding extra anxiety since they had no idea of the man's true identity.

"For a moment there," said Dr. Kastleboro to Ms. Willoughby, "I was wishing our actor really was Leonardo da Vinci. That would make me feel safer."

Ms. Willoughby looked puzzled and said nothing.

"I guess I have no one but myself to blame," said Dr. Kastleboro. "After all, I did bring him into our trip. I thought it would be fun, but this isn't fun."

"Well, if they don't show up shortly, we'll have to call their parents as well as the local police," said Ms. Willoughby, silently praying that the students weren't in trouble or harmed.

As they walked into the open area of the piazza, a black Maserati passed them, drove across to the other side to the corner of the Uffizi, and stopped. The incident drew the attention of people wandering nearby. A number of men wearing black suits with brightly colored sashes across their chests, officials of the Florence government, rushed to the rear door of the vehicle. As it opened, the teachers were surprised to see Leonardo da Vinci emerge from the back seat. He was followed by the mayor, but not the students.

"I'm not sure if that's a good sign or a bad one," said Dr. Kastleboro uncertainly.

℘℃℞

During the drive from the airport, the mayor explained what he wanted from Leonardo.

"You see," said the mayor to Leonardo as the car sped smoothly along the highway. "The truth of the matter is, I don't think for a moment that you are really Leonardo da Vinci returned from the dead. I don't know who you are, but you are an excellent actor. Maybe you're seeking the Florence culture to ready yourself for a play or a movie, but regardless, we have a plan."

Leonardo was surprised. He had taken the man at his word when he said that he was being welcomed back after 500 years. He assumed there was no question of his authenticity. Now there seemed to be a different purpose. He felt annoyance, then anger at the deception.

Leonardo frowned, stroking his beard and studying the man beside him. He said, "I'm afraid, good sir, I don't understand."

"If you are as real as you claim, then you owe something to Florence. When the real Leonardo da Vinci left Florence to travel to Milan to meet the man who would later become the king of France, he left behind an unfinished painting for which the Signoria had paid him hundreds of florins—gold florins at that."

Why is he talking about that fresco? wondered Leonardo.

"If you are talking about the mural of the *Battle of Anghiari*, I did as much work on it as I could. After I prepared the sketch, I outlined the entire drawing on the wall in the Hall of Five Hundred. The Signoria was to provide me with the supplies I needed, particularly linseed oil. Unfortunately, they purchased

113

the cheapest oil they could find. It was defective, but I couldn't tell until after I had used it.

"After I applied the first layer of paint, it would not dry. I tried to hasten the drying process by cloaking the painting area with giant curtains and then lighting candles to throw heat on the wall. In the heat, however, the paint began to melt and run down the wall. I could not paint over it until it dried. So, I waited for it to dry. Before I could continue, I was summoned to Milan."

"But, Mr. da Vinci, we can't find your mural. We are bringing you back to find and finish it, or, better still, to have you paint a new one for us."

"I do not mind painting even though it has been many centuries since I last held a brush. I certainly would welcome the opportunity to return to my art, but regrettably, I must say no to your offer. I have an obligation, or rather a need, to learn."

"And why is that?" asked the mayor in a voice of amusement.

"I must use my considerable talents to invent or discover something to better mankind."

The mayor tried to keep mockery out of his voice. "What kind of discovery or invention do you have in mind?"

"Well, that is my problem. It must be new, and yet I am just learning that the things I envisioned for the future have already been invented. I need help to find a quest worthy of my efforts."

Leonardo could tell that the mayor was being glib and had no interest in helping him. He regretted abandoning the students, who seemed to be the only ones who believed and understood who he was.

Leonardo prodded the mayor, saying, "Perhaps you could introduce me to some learned university professors."

"The painting must come first."

"Please, sir," said Leonardo, trying to make this man understand the absurdity of the request. "Could you tell me why that painting of the Battle of Angahari is so important? In my trip in the airplane, I had the opportunity to look down on Florence, Pisa, and Siena. The walls are down or abandoned. There surely are no more wars between these cities or even with the city of

Milan against which city the Battle of Anghiari was fought. Who will care about that battle?

"Besides, even though Florence won, the battle was actually fought by paid mercenary soldiers on both sides. The truth of the matter was that the soldiers fought each other well enough, and the Florence forces won the day, but the mercenary soldiers certainly weren't interested in getting killed for Florence. In fact, nobody on either side was killed except for one man who fell off his horse. The great Battle of Anghiari was just shouting and pushing and shoving. All show. More of a sporting event than a war."

"Then why were you hired to paint a mural in honor of the victory?"

"Because at that time, it was good publicity for Florence." Leonardo looked pointedly at the mayor. "In those days, very few people could read. From what I am able to observe of this century, most people can read. But in my previous lifetime, a painting on a public wall was a good way for people to remember great historical events. The fresco was intended to create pride in our city."

The mayor stifled a laugh. *Yes*, he thought, *publicity and pride for Florence is a good idea, no matter the century.* "Look," he said, "maybe finishing that painting isn't all that important now, but I need to ask you to say or do something at the piazza."

"Say what? To whom?"

"Something to the council members and whoever else might be there to show that you have truly returned to Florence."

"You mean," Leonardo said bitterly, "that I am really Leonardo da Vinci, and not a fake?"

"Of course," said the mayor, realizing suddenly that pretending to believe him would get more cooperation. Changing his tone of voice, the mayor continued. "There is no honor in celebrating a look-alike, a performer. But if you really are Leonardo da Vinci, then the return of Florence's greatest citizen is an occasion to celebrate."

Leonardo had no way to judge this man. As the leader of the city, he was the right man to introduce him to important men of science, but Leonardo suspected he was not going to aid him in his quest. Still he decided to press his opportunity. "In exchange, will you introduce me to learned professors at a university?"

The mayor looked at Leonardo. "Certainly," he said. Seeing Leonardo's hand on the seat next to him. He was struck by the idea that he should try to get his guest's fingerprints so that they could be checked through Interpol. As the Maserati drove slowly through the narrow streets, the mayor used his car phone to arrange for a glass of Chianti for Leonardo.

Soon, the car pulled into the Piazza della Signoria. They approached the arch-fronted and statue-filled covered area at the rear of the Uffizi that functioned as a stage for the piazza. When they reached the stage, they stopped in front of the steps leading to the middle arched area, where Leonardo da Vinci stepped out of the automobile.

He was immediately handed a glass of wine. He accepted the glass thankfully and consumed the wine in a single gulp. Then he handed the glass back to the gloved man. The mayor smiled, thinking *Gotcha! With those fingerprints, we'll find out who you are soon enough.*

As Leonardo and the mayor walked up the steps to the platform in his wake, multiple members of the men on the stage held black objects toward his face. The tourists in the piazza did not know what to make of the proceedings. They assumed that some form of ceremony or celebration was taking place and stayed to enjoy it as part of the romance and charm of the old city. As they watched, a tall, blond, full-bearded man in brand new khakis and a brown leather bomber jacket was being guided up the steps to the platform by officials.

They applauded without knowing why except that it seemed appropriate.

On the platform, the mayor bowed and, taking a microphone handed to him by Antonio Gigliardi, nodded to the nearby television cameras. Speaking in his most official voice, he said, "Ladies and gentlemen, welcome to Florence, the flower-seed of the Renaissance! Florence, the city that lit the darkness! Throughout the day, there has been some attention given to what may be a remarkable and historic event, a miracle of our time... you may be witnessing the miraculous return to Florence of the famous Leonardo da Vinci!"

Here, he swept one arm out toward Leonardo. "This gentleman standing next to me claims to be Leonardo da Vinci, returned from the dead to visit us again after a 500-year absence from the city of his fame, Florence."

His brief statement in Italian was repeated in English by an interpreter, and then again in Japanese. There was an audible response from the crowd—part cheer, part moan, part laughter.

"We will continue to translate," said the mayor, "as I ask Mr. da Vinci to introduce himself."

Leonardo looked around. He was not a stranger to playing to an audience. He had often been called upon to be an organizer, director, and master of ceremony for pageants for Duke Ludovico in Milan. The gathered crowd grew quiet, straining to hear as he asked the mayor, "How does one use this device?"

At first, the mayor did not understand the question.

Then he realized the actor was referring to the microphone. So, he answered dramatically, hamming up the moment. *Pretending to not understand how to use the microphone—this actor really knew his business.* "This is a microphone, Mr. da Vinci. It is a miracle of these modern times, created to enhance any performance or speech. All the greats are using them these days. One merely holds it thus," he demonstrated, "and speaks directly into the top. It will amplify your voice so all present can hear what you have to say."

"We can't hear you!" someone from the crowd shouted. Those near the front, who had heard the quiet conversation between Leonardo and the mayor, were grinning.

"How does it do that?" Leonardo asked, taking the microphone.

"Electricity," said the mayor.

"That magic force," murmured Leonardo.

The mayor, who hadn't heard what Leonardo said, continued, "Go ahead, Mr. da Vinci. Talk into the microphone. We are all curious about what wisdom you have to share."

"Yes." Hesitating as he considered what he was going to say. "*Buon giorno, cittadini di Firenze*. I am Leonardo da Vinci." There was some hesitant applause. "Your *Gonfaloniere* has referred me to you as Mr. da Vinci. I am not Mr. da Vinci!" He paused.

The mayor's heart leapt—was the man about to reveal his true identity? The gathered crowd grew hushed.

Then Leonardo explained. "Vinci is the town where I grew up, where I am from. I am Leonardo from the town of Vinci. When I was apprenticed here in Florence, no one would have called me Mr. da Vinci. Most people of my time called me Leonardo." He grinned and waited for a small pocket of laughter.

"When I became famous, I was called Maestro. I would be pleased to be so addressed now." A few more people in the crowd laughed, but the laughter was short-lived, as most wanted to listen. This was a performance they wanted to hear.

⁊⊙⍩

Meanwhile, Tad was carefully guiding the golf cart through the streets and around large groups of pedestrians. The crowds grew thicker as they approached the Ponte Vecchio.

"I hope we're not too late," said Gina.

"Oh, I'm sure he can handle matters without us," said Max, concentrating on the directions the professor had given them to make sure they were going the right way.

⁊⊙⍩

In the piazza, a television announcer with a camera focused on Leonardo described the event. "This is Guy Parkinson, with CNN, broadcasting from the heart of historic Florence, Italy, the birthplace of the Renaissance. Here in the rolling green hills of the magnificent Tuscan countryside, we are about to either witness the greatest miracle of this new century or a performance by one of the best impersonation actors in Europe. On the platform, with the mayor of Florence and members of the council, is the man who claims to be Leonardo da Vinci, returned to life to offer his services to humankind. And considering the shape the world is in, we could sure use some from the likes of Leonardo da Vinci, *if* he is the real McCoy—no, wait, make that the real da Vinci!"

On the platform by the Uffizi, Leonardo continued his show. "If I were to tell you that I have been given a second chance at life in order to use my special talents to invent something or to make a discovery to benefit mankind, you might mock me…"

"You got that right, partner," came a voice from the crowd. Since it was said in English, the remark went unnoticed by Leonardo.

"…but I would prefer that you, all of you, help direct me to some great need that has not been met or some problem that I can solve."

The entire crowd began to laugh.

In the background there was a mixture of voices from several TV announcers describing the event.

From the audience, another voice shouted in Italian, "Hey, Maestro, if you came from the great beyond, could you tell us the winning lottery numbers on tomorrow's drawing?"

There was even more laughter. Leonardo was puzzled and unsure of what he should say or do.

"Hey, he's all talk and no action!" came another shout from the crowd when Leonardo remained silent.

Antonio Gigliardi had anticipated this moment. From the back of the platform, he lifted an easel, set it up, and placed a large, white poster on it. "Here, Maestro," he said. "Show us who you are." He handed Leonardo a thick black crayon.

Leonardo looked at the poster and then at the crayon.

He felt the texture of the crayon and tentatively tested it on the edge of the poster board. "Excellent drawing tool," he said. Then, ignoring the mayor, the crayon, and the white poster, he lifted the microphone again to his mouth. "For one thing," said Leonardo, "this voice magnification device is a marvel. I would have loved to have such a machine 500 years ago."

Then, smiling at his audience, he began to sing. Very few students who had studied Leonardo ever focused on the fact that he was a great musician and, even more, a talented singer. He had sung often to soothe his subjects as he painted, particularly the rich or famous ones. At first, no one heard him. Then his voice grew louder. Suddenly, in a burst of vocal power amplified by the microphone, he sang a Latin Catholic hymn, an ancient Gregorian Chant: *Dies Irae*, or *The Day of Wrath*. He had perfect pitch. The clarity of his voice and the sacredness of this particular chant brought a reverent hush over the entire piazza.

No one spoke as he continued to sing the chant. It was a hymn that was usually sung by a choir of both men and women. When Leonardo sang the women's part, he sang in a tenor voice, and for the men's part, he sang in baritone.

As he sang, more people crowded into the piazza to see what was happening. "Listen to that voice," they whispered. "He is *incredible*."

As he was singing and holding the microphone in his right hand, he tested the crayon along the top of the board using his left hand. The crayon was not paint and not charcoal, but it felt smooth and presented an easy and pleasing black line. All of a sudden, in short, swift movements, he drew a single-line drawing, a caricature of the mayor, with an extra large nose and a sharp, pointed chin and the body of a cherub, displaying undersized angel wings.

While he held the audience in awe, those who were close enough to see what he was drawing began to snicker. The mayor was smiling at the crowd and did not notice the cartoon. The television cameras hummed and individual cameras flashed.

೮)ೞ

At the same time, the three students passed the Ponte Vecchio. Tad shouted Italian warnings provided to him by Gina.

"Attento! Attento!
Ci passa!
Spostare tuo grosso derrier!"
They slowly eased through the mass of tourists as paths opened before them in response to Tad's shouts.

When they reached the edge of the piazza, they were puzzled to hear singing. As soon as they entered the piazza and saw the vocalist, though, they hurried.

෪෨

Next, writing from right to left in his signature left-handed, backward, mirror scrawl, Leonardo wrote words nobody could read. Being a man with a great sense of humor, he began to warm to his task. He continued the chant, singing both parts while making caricatures with his left hand.

Next, he sketched the Vitruvian Man, arms outstretched, superimposed in a circle within a square. However, instead of the slender, muscular body of the Vitruvian Man, he drew a fat, flabby man with skinny legs and capped him with the exaggerated, cartoon face of Antonio Gigliardi, who was too busy talking to his cameraman to notice. By now, the nearby crowd was roaring with laughter.

Finally, on the space he had left on the lower left side of the white poster, Leonardo sketched three grappling horses and riders as he had sketched them 500 years ago as the centerpiece on his original painting of the Battle of Anghiari. Only, instead of armed warriors grappling in mortal combat to retrieve the flag of victory, he placed a man and woman on two of the horses and had them kissing each other. The crowd went wild.

Giuseppe leaned over to the mayor and shouted into his ear over the roar of the crowd. "This is better than I thought it would be! This guy is good. It doesn't matter that he is phony through and through. He is a great act. All of the world will think about Florence and the richness of our history and our artistic culture. Millions will hear this, see these sketches and the TV drama, and come here. The sketches by this guy are good, really good. He must be a street artist as well as a performer."

The mayor turned to look at what had been drawn.

He gasped. "Tony!" he shouted over the roar of the crowd. "Do you see what he drew?"

"Yeah. Don't care. They love it. This has turned into a great event. This actor can hold a crowd."

"He drew you and me!"

Antonio nodded toward the board and whooped. Then he chuckled. "This guy is remarkable. Looks just like both of us, only prettier."

The mayor did not share his sense of humor. "Libel," he muttered.

"It goes with your rank and station," Antonio said in a mocking tone. "The guy's entertaining for free; he's entitled to a few small indulgences. Besides, I can frame this as a personal drawing by 'Leonardo da Vinci.' I'll be rich."

Leonardo finished the chant, bowed to the crowd, and turned back to the mayor. "Now, will you take me to a university and introduce me to learned professors? I am not an entertainer. I am a scientist."

Meanwhile, the large crowd that jammed into the piazza was cheering and applauding wildly, chanting for more.

"Oh, yes, you want to meet professors," said the mayor. "Right now, we can't just leave this crowd and it's late. We'll go to the university first thing tomorrow. But right now, why don't you sing another song? Come on, one more song?"

Leonardo didn't like it, but he nodded, thinking that this man was more likely than the teenagers to be able to introduce him to someone who could help him. They were so young, and they weren't even from Florence. How would they know anyone who could help? How would they get him to a university to meet professors? As much as he didn't like the mayor, the man was in a position to help. He began another song.

From across the piazza, Dr. Kastleboro and Ms Willoughby watched the parade of events while trying to figure out a plan for continuing their search.

Pondering their next action, Dr. Kastleboro said, "That actor's certainly getting the attention he wanted from the important people of Florence."

"Oh, I don't know," said Ms. Willoughby. "I'm not so sure that this is what he wanted."

"Then why would he be singing for this huge crowd if he didn't crave attention?"

"I don't know," she said, looking thoughtful.

Just at that moment, they spotted a golf cart with "Firenze Ugolina Circola Golf" stenciled along the side. It appeared out of the crowd and headed toward Leonardo.

"Look," Ms. Willoughby screamed. "It's the kids! They're driving that cart!"

"What in the world!?"

"Where'd they get a golf cart?" Ms. Willoughby asked, perplexed. "Hurry! We need to reach them."

Dr. Kastleboro began to push through the crowd, followed closely by Ms. Willoughby. "Tad, Gina, Max! Wait! Stop!" They both shouted, trying to catch their students' attention over the buzz of the crowd. But they were too far away to be heard and the crowd was too dense for them to be seen.

From their cart, the three students could see Leonardo with the microphone and hear him singing. The entire scene was puzzling to them.

"We need to get him to go with us," said Gina.

"How?" Tad was barely able to continue moving the cart as they approached the crowd, which was pressing around the platform.

"Follow me!" hollered Max over the mixture of the noise of the people and Leonardo's singing. He leaped from the rear of the cart, grabbed Gina's hand and guided her toward the stage.

Meanwhile, Dr. Kastleboro and Ms. Willoughby pushed through the crowd from the other side of the piazza.

Max, who, as a short kid, was used to squeezing through crowds, successfully made his way toward the stage, "Maestro! Maestro!" he shouted.

Leonardo turned toward the voice he recognized and tried to see Max through the crowd.

"Da questa parte!" yelled Gina. "Over here! Maestro, we are going to take you to Florence University!"

In spite of the noise of the crowd, the teachers could hear Max and Gina shouting, so they began to shout for their charges.

Leonardo, at that moment, looking toward the voices, could see Gina and Max squeezing between the crowds.

He stopped singing. *"Che cosa? Che cosa?"* he shouted back.

"L'università!" repeated Gina. "We have an appointment for you to meet Professor Montebello. He can help you."

"Si?" responded Leonardo. *"Si!"* With that, he dropped the microphone and reached out for Max and Gina.

The mayor caught the microphone cord and grabbed at Leonardo. "No! Stop! You must finish!"

"Whoa! What do you think you're doing?" added Antonio Gigliardi to Leonardo. "You can't leave now. You must consider the magic of this moment. International television cameras are broadcasting this event around the world!"

Leonardo, confused by the mixture of voices and commands, quickly realized that his only hope was in trusting the three teenagers. He yanked free from the mayor and Gigliardi. *"Aspetta, gonfaloniere, i bambini sono venuti a salvarmi,"* said Leonardo, letting them know that he was leaving with the kids.

Dr. Kastleboro and Ms Willoughby cried, "Wait! Stop where you are!"

Leonardo reached toward Max and Gina while hurrying down the concrete steps.

The audience, shocked by the sudden end to the chant and the fun of the drawings, also began to shout. "What's happening?" The roar of voices in English, Italian, Japanese and other languages were all blurring together. Some people tried to reach and grab the khaki-clad, bearded entertainer.

Max saw the people grabbing at Leonardo, and at the same time, the two teachers pressing toward them. He knew they were shouting for them to stop, but since their voices could not be heard over the boisterous crowd he looked away and pretended not to see or hear them.

He and Gina cleared a path for their prize. As they reached the golf cart, Max leaned over to Tad and shouted into Tad's ear. "Hurry, Tad, the cavalry is trying to cut us off at the pass!"

"What the...?" Tad muttered as he turned and saw Dr. Kastleboro and Ms. Willoughby. Understanding the situation, he also pretended he had not seen them. There was no time to lose. They would explain later. They had to get the Maestro away from the officials and to the university where real academic help awaited. Turning the golf cart around quickly, Tad paused momentarily as his two classmates and Leonardo da Vinci grabbed the upright pipes and swung into the passenger seats. As they did, Tad pressed the pedal to the floor. The golf cart lurched wildly forward and gained speed.

As they pressed out of the crowd, Tad resumed shouting: *"Attento! Attento! Ci passa! Spostare tuo grosso derrier!!"*

Some people in the crowd shook their fists and responded in menacing Italian, quickly moving out of the way of the racing golf cart. Closing in, Dr. Kastleboro and Ms. Willoughby broke through the crowd and stretched their hands out toward the students while shouting their names.

Two stumbling spectators, trying to keep up with the action twisted, lost their balance and fell into the teachers, allowing enough extra time for Tad to race toward the corner of the piazza as if he had not noticed them approaching.

"What the devil?" said Dr. Kastleboro, red-faced in anger.

"I think they heard us and ignored us," said Ms. Willoughby sharing her fellow teacher's anger.

As the golf cart pulled away with gaining speed, Dr. Kastleboro and Ms. Willoughby stopped their pursuit.

"Well," said Dr. Kastleboro in a calmer, but still angry, voice, "at least we know they are unharmed."

"And," she added, catching her breath, momentarily smiling, "we also know where they're going and who they're meeting, a Professor Montebello, whoever he is." Then triumphantly, "They're gone for now, but we'll find them at the University of Florence."

Passing behind the buildings and around the corner, Tad, Max, Gina, and Leonardo now rolled easily toward their destination.

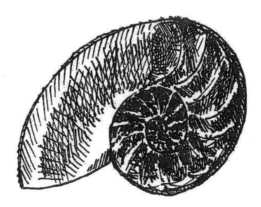

11. A LESSON LEARNED

Rolling swiftly, Tad guided the golf cart toward the university. Some tourists waved as they passed, others shook their fists angrily as Tad shouted in Italian at those blocking his way.

"Hey Gina, what do, *'Attento, Ci passa,'* and *'Spostare tuo grosso derrier'* mean?"

She smiled at his question. "What you are saying is 'Watch out' and 'Coming through.'"

"Fair enough," said Tad.

Then giggling, she added, "And 'move your big fat butt!'"

Tad glared at her. "Seriously? That's what I've been shouting?"

"Si," she replied, trying to look contrite.

Tad laughed. "So thoughtful of us to be guests in another country and then insult the locals. You know, Gina, you could've gotten us killed!"

Leonardo interrupted. "Thank you. Thank you. I am so grateful to you three for helping me escape in this amazing flowing cart. And I am excited to be heading toward a university. I am now hopeful."

"You should be," answered Gina, happy for the adventure, but still feeling the sting of annoyance at having been abandoned at the hanger. "You, know, Maestro, you left us without transportation at the airport."

"Yes, I realize that," said Leonardo, feeling guilty. "It was selfish and wrong. I am truly sorry and I hope you will forgive me."

Feeling better with an apology, Gina suddenly realized that she had a unique opportunity to pose a question that she was sure many people would like to ask. "The *Mona Lisa*, Maestro," she said, "as an apology, tell us everything: why you painted it, what she meant to you, and how you created such a painting that has captured the admiration of the entire world."

"What do you know about the *Mona Lisa*?"

"It's a painting I studied in school. I know it's quite small and of a medieval woman with what many consider an indefinable smile that has mystified people for hundreds of years. Today, it is considered one of the most famous paintings in the world and hangs all by itself on its own wall in Paris, France, in the Louvre, the most famous art gallery in the world. Art experts have been arguing about it for years, trying to understand why you painted the *Mona Lisa* and to decipher what her smile means." When she stopped, she blew out the breath she was holding in during her rapid-fire speech.

"My," said Leonardo, "that is quite a recital. Very well. I do owe you. What I'm about to tell you is unknown to anyone else. I did not write down in my notes any of these facts I'm about to reveal. What I tell you is private, but I suppose after five hundred years, keeping it hidden doesn't matter anymore.

"When I first returned to Florence from Milan after being away for sixteen years, all of Florence was raving about this new young artist and sculptor, Michelangelo, just as they had once raved about me. Oh, his work was quite good, but it did not match my own." He flicked his hand as if to brush away inferior art. "At that time, I was looking for a commission to paint something, anything, in order to replenish my dwindling fortunes. The Signoria, the governing body of Florence, employed me to paint a mural of the great Battle of Anghiari, fought between the armies of Milan and the armies of Florence, or maybe between Florence and Pisa. Oh, no matter. The painting was to be a reminder to the citizens of some great victory."

"A reminder? Was there a great victory?" asked Gina, grabbing onto the seat as Tad jerkily accelerated through an opening in the crowd."

"Not really," he answered. "But since so few people could read or write, a visual reminder was important. The painting was to be on the wall of the Hall of Five Hundred. On the opposite wall, Michelangelo was commissioned to paint the *Battle of Cascina*, an equally famous battle between the armies of Florence and Siena."

"Why these battles?" asked Tad after Gina finished translating.

"The city-states were always fighting with each other. Neither Michelangelo nor I ever really completed our paintings, although I finished a central part of the painting that was to become a mural on the wall. I would have finished the whole thing if I had not been supplied with defective oil." He paused, and stared into the distance as he drew upon his memory.

"And the *Mona Lisa?*" Gina reminded him.

"Ah, yes. Mona Lisa Gherardini *la Giocondo*. She was the lovely and beautiful wife of Francesco del Giocondo. While I was painting the battle scene, I became friendly with Francesco. He was a kindly man and I liked him a great deal. His grand house stood across the Piazza Santa Maria Novella near the Hall where I was working. During that time, I met Mona Lisa, his third wife. He was much older than she. When he married her, she was only fifteen years old and an extremely beautiful girl. Her beauty filled any room she entered. Spectacular. Overwhelming.

"Within a few years after their marriage, she bore a daughter to whom she was devoted. Her daughter was even more beautiful. She loved her little girl and doted upon her with tremendous love and attention. Unfortunately, the child suffered a sudden and tragic death.

"Following the death of her daughter, Mona Lisa fell into a deep melancholy. Her sadness was understandable, yet she carried her sorrow with remarkable grace. It was this over-whelming grief that was etched by her beauty into a vision that I felt only a true artist could see. This special beauty was to me something divine. I know that in a quiet, private way, I loved her, and as an artist, I needed to capture the poignant and celestial beauty she radiated. I knew that the inevitable march of time would wrinkle her flesh and that finally death would remove her face from the memory of all who had known her. Her beauty would be lost forever. I could not let that happen. Only a painting, and only a painting by me, could preserve her face for all times. That sounds vain, but I knew my talents. I was the best." Once again, he stared into the space of his memory as they drove along.

"I loved that painting just as I loved her, and I continued to work on it over the years. When I was summoned from Florence by the man who would later become the king of France and whose armies had just conquered Milan, Francesco del Giocondo considered the painting to be finished and wished to pay me and keep it in Florence. But it was not finished, so I carried it with me."

"I thought Milan was at war with Florence," said Gina.

He laughed. "No. In those days, wars came and went according to which duke or other ruler was in charge. Sides changed often and without much sense. A royal marriage, for instance, could change alliances. Mostly, it was about the force of arms and the power of money and commerce.

"On this peninsula, the great city-states of Florence, Milan, and Venice held the ultimate power in the north, while the Roman Catholic Church and Naples held the power in the south. My own loyalties unfortunately depended upon the need for my services as a painter, architect, military engineer, hydraulic expert or even carnival designer. In reality, I went with whoever could pay for my services. I needed commissions and fees in order to support myself as well as my assistants and servants. In spite of my monetary problems, the *Mona Lisa* painting belonged to me and went with me. Over the years,

I continued to make painting adjustments. After a while, it became much more to me than just a portrait of Mona Lisa Gherardini—it became a vision of my own soul.

"After I returned to Milan, I added background to the painting—the rocky landscape and the waterways at a precise point on the Adda at Paderno that was transfixed in my mind, along with the brittle blue skies of Lombardy." Leonardo leaned toward Gina. "Now you tell me: why would you, a teenage girl, be focused on one simple portrait out of all the art that has been produced over the centuries? Why the portrait of Mona Lisa Gherardini?"

"Well," said Gina thoughtfully, pushing her flying hair away from her face. "I think everybody has a reason to admire that painting. I, for one, love the mystery that many find in her smile. It is sad, yet calm and all-knowing. When I was younger, I felt that love had been added like a color." Gina stopped suddenly, a bit embarrassed. "But, hey, let's ask the guys."

"Then ask them," said Leonardo nodding toward Tad.

After she translated, Tad said, "We studied that painting in school. I just thought it was a painting of a lady who was sad because she was growing old."

Max said, "And I liked it because I could see that you acquired the pleasing balance in the painting by using two mathematical formulas."

"Math?" said Gina and Tad together. She then translated for Leonardo.

Upon hearing Max's remark, he brightened and said, "Yes, math. Mathematical formulas." He paused and studied Max, who was always so neat and precise in his white shirt, his red bow tie and dark-rimmed glasses. "Well, young man, you are right."

"What are you talking about, Max? What does math have to do with the *Mona Lisa*?" asked Tad.

"I saw it the first time I saw a picture of the *Mona Lisa*."

"What, Max?" Tad turned from driving to glance at his friend. They swerved a bit and Gina pointed to the road to remind Tad to pay attention as he drove.

"There are two famous math concepts in one single painting."

"He is correct," Leonardo said to Gina after she translated Max's remark.

"Tell us, Max," said Gina.

Max smiled. "Her portrait lies entirely within a golden rectangle, and the total presentation of Mona Lisa's body and facial position in the frame of the painting makes her mouth and her smile the focus of the painting by the proportions of the Golden Spiral."

"What are you talking about?" asked Tad.

"The Golden Spiral is a graphic representation of the Fibonacci Sequence," Max explained, waving his hands and squaring his thumbs and fingers as he attempted to demonstrate his point.

Following Gina's translation, Leonardo clapped his hands in approval. "Now *that*, young man, is impressive and entirely correct. Not many people could pick up that point."

"You're going to have to explain it to us, Max," said Gina, repeating in English what Leonardo said.

"Okay," Max began. "The Golden Rectangle is a rectangle of any size, big or small, so long as the ratio between its length and width matches the exact proportions of 1 to 1.618. That means if the width of a rectangle is one foot long, then the length would have to be 1.618 feet long. No one can explain why those proportions are special, but they seem to be pleasing to look at. Many famous buildings are designed to take advantage of the pleasing nature of the Golden Rectangle.

"The most famous is the Parthenon in Ancient Greece, but the Golden Rectangle is not limited to buildings—it is also apparent in other forms of art. For example, the Maestro used the Golden Rectangle in painting the *Mona Lisa*."

"How?" Tad asked, turning left at Gina's direction.

"As I just explained, the entire frame of the painting is a Golden Rectangle. Look at the ratio between the height of the frame as contrasted to the width of the frame. That is obvious. But what is not obvious is that Mona Lisa's portrait is in the proportions of a Golden Rectangle."

Max smiled at his companions. He loved having their attention. More than that, he loved having an audience when describing the magic of mathematics. "There are two amazing things about a Golden Rectangle. First, if you draw a square inside of a Golden Rectangle, the remaining piece will itself be a smaller Golden Rectangle."

Tad and Gina stared at Max. "What? They both are?"

"Let me draw an example." Writing on his notebook, which he lifted from the small satchel he always carried, he drew a rectangle. "Now, suppose this rectangle is exactly one foot wide and 1.618 feet long. If I draw a line from top to bottom exactly one foot from one side, I will make a square one foot by one foot. This will set the stage for the formation of a Golden Spiral. Go ahead, try the geometry."

"Not us," said Tad.

Leonardo watched Max draw the standard example and nodded with pleasure.

"And," said Max, "the second amazing thing is this— if we take this same drawing of the Golden Rectangle and find the point in the exact middle of the bottom line of this square I just made, and then from that middle point draw a straight line up to the right hand corner of the square, you will see we have made a right triangle—you know, a triangle in which one angle is ninety degrees. The longest line of that triangle will be the line we just drew from the middle of the lower line of the square up to the top right corner. That, of course, is the hypotenuse."

"Hypotenuse?" said Tad. "That line is a hypotenuse? Wow, I thought a hypotenuse was a dark brown animal with a round snout that lived in rivers in the jungle." He laughed.

"That's a hippopotamus," Gina told him. "You're silly."

"Now," Max continued. "If you treat that long line—the hypotenuse—as the radius of a circle, and draw another circle using that point in the middle of the lower line of the square circling from the top end of the line to draw the circumference of the circle, that circumference will cut through exactly at the bottom right hand corner of the original Golden Rectangle."

"What does all that mean?" asked Gina.

"Ask the Maestro," said Max.

After he had been asked, Leonardo said, "It illustrates how mathematics, when presented graphically, can produce a pleasing presentation. That's why I used it in the *Mona Lisa* painting."

"Then what about the Golden Spiral?" Gina asked Max.

"Ah, that's a little more complicated," Max replied. "You can see the Golden Spiral in the expanding spirals in nature like the spirals of a pine cone or of a sunflower and most dramatically in a nautilus sea shell. It is a presentation of the Fibonacci Sequence."

"Ugh," groaned Tad. "This is worse than I thought. This is like being in school, except I don't understand what Max just said."

"No, it's not like being in school—it's way better," said Max before he turned to Gina. "Could you ask Maestro if he could help me explain the Fibonacci Sequence?"

When Leonardo heard the request, he shook his head and said to Gina, "No, your young scholar friend can do it, I am sure. He could not have seen it in the painting if he did not know about the rabbits."

"Rabbits?" laughed Tad after Gina translated. "Is this going to be like the hippopotamus?"

"No," said Max, "the rabbits were rabbits. But rabbits were the inspiration for the basis for the most famous mathematician of medieval times to present the Fibonacci Sequence. Leonardo Pisano Fibonacci, a young man from Pisa, wrote a book in the early 13th century called *Liber Abaci*. I have never seen a copy of that book, but I did learn about the rabbits and the Fibonacci Sequence."

"Max, what does this have to do with rabbits?" asked Gina.

"Numbers were his thing. In *Liber Abaci*, Fibonacci posed a mathematical problem."

"What problem?"

"Well, if you start with a single pair of rabbits, how many pairs of rabbits will be produced in a year if each pair of rabbits gives birth to a new pair of rabbits every month followed by the new pairs becoming productive beginning in the next month and so on? From this problem, he produced the famous Fibonacci Sequence, which is simply a series of numbers in which each of two previous numbers are added together to produce the next number. Here is the sequence: 1, 1, 2, 3, 5, 8, 13, 21, 34, 55, 89, 144, 233…"

"I still don't get it," Tad complained. He stopped at an intersection and waited for the pedestrians to cross.

"Simple, we add up the sequential numbers: $1 + 1 = 2$; then $1 + 2 = 3$; then $2 + 3 = 5$; then $3 + 5 = 8$; then $5 + 8 = 13$, and so on and so forth as far as you wish to count. In the rabbit case, he only counted one year twelve times to determine that he would have 233 rabbits at the end of a year. This is called a recursive sequence. When visualized, it looks like a spiraling line. It's very visually appealing, and it's seen everywhere in nature—on sea shells and pine cones, in the petals of flowers and the shape of beehives, in the spiral of hurricanes, and even, of the galaxy. Why that sequence is found in nature, I don't know. Maybe someday I'll find the answer. In the *Mona Lisa* painting, an imaginary spiral over her face draws the viewer's eyes to her smile tightly and gracefully."

As the number of tourists began to thin, Tad was able to pick up speed and soon they caught sight of the trees filling the Piazza di San Marco.

12. THE UNIVERSITY

"There it is, Maestro," said Tad as Gina translated.

Within a few minutes, they were at the front of the university. The street was narrow, but there were still bicycles and motor scooters parked against the building and in front of the arched entrance door of the stone building. Tad pulled the golf cart as close as he could to the curb along the narrow street.

The moment of their arrival was heralded by the simultaneous arrival of a white Fiat with a broad blue stripe bearing the words, "POLIZIA MUNICIPALE," along the side and a flashing blue light across the top.

"Now what?" asked Tad.

The police car pulled close to them, stopped, and an officer in a blue uniform with a white, military-peaked cap exited the car. He walked slowly and deliberately toward the golf cart, looking carefully at the stenciled lettering along the side before facing Leonardo, who sat in the rear of the cart.

"Well," said the officer in Italian to Leonardo, "you must have had a lousy golf game. You're way off of the fairway."

Leonardo da Vinci eyed him warily. *"Mi scusi. Non capisco,"* responded Leonardo, shrugging his shoulders.

The officer placed his foot on one of the wheels and leaned in toward Leonardo. "Okay, *Signore*, maybe it will help if you tell me why you and your children are riding around Florence in this golf cart which obviously belongs to the Cirolo Golf Ugolina."

"These are not my children," said Leonardo shaking his head, "They are students and my friends, and this is their marvelous horseless cart."

"Marvelous horseless cart," said the officer mocking Leonardo. Cocking his head to one side, he repeated, "Marvelous horseless cart. Oh, this is rich. *Signore,* who are you anyway?"

Gina started to speak, but the officer motioned her to be quiet by holding up his hand.

"I am Leonardo da Vinci," said Leonardo.

The police officer chuckled. Then he said, *"Si, e io sono il Papa.* Right, and I'm the Pope."

"The pope? How many popes are there now?" asked Leonardo.

Gina, bouncing in the front seat of the golf cart and waving her hands in front of Leonardo, interrupted, and in Italian, said, "Wait, please. Maestro, this man is a police officer questioning the ownership of the cart. He thinks it is stolen. Please, let me." Then turning to the officer, she said, "This cart was loaned to us by Professor Montebello and we're here at the university to meet him."

The police officer eyed her carefully. He recognized that the Italian spoken by the girl identified her as an American, while the bearded man's Italian was stiff and from an older generation. *Something was definitely strange about this group.* "The famous Professor Ludwig Montebello, eh? He is well known here in Florence. So," he said, "why don't we all just march into this building and let Professor Montebello tell me the real story, personally. If he does not verify your story, we'll talk some more down at the station."

It was a strange single-file troop, led by the police officer that trailed slowly through the dark wooden front doors of the building. It smelled of education—the aroma of aging paint, musty alcoves and old books. They found Professor Montebello's name on the directory and followed the winding corridors to his second floor office.

When they knocked, a voice boomed out, "I hope you didn't wreck my cart. Please come in."

Professor Montebello was surprised when the first person to enter his office was a police officer. "What? Has there been an accident?" he exclaimed, rising from behind the desk where he had been working. Gina, Tad, Max, and Leonardo all followed behind the officer.

Professor Montebello's office was cramped and filled with stacks of books, manuscripts, and a litter of unopened mail. It was a tight squeeze for all of them to find a place to stand.

The officer asked, "Are you Professor Montebello?" The professor smiled, "It has been accurately reported that I am."

"These people claim that you loaned them a golf cart and invited them to a meeting here. And the bearded guy here claims to be the long-dead Leonardo da Vinci. Is any part of this true?"

Professor Montebello chuckled. "The part about the cart and the invitation is true. The rest depends on this meeting I'm about to have with the bearded gentleman."

"Well," said the officer shrugging his shoulders and easing his way out of the door. "No arrests, just a good station house story. Good luck, Professor. I thought we might be dealing with a stolen vehicle, so I'm done. I'm glad everything is okay. As for this Leonardo da Vinci business—well, my duties include traffic enforcement, but the return of dead people is well above my pay grade. Go enjoy your meeting."

Leonardo, following the Italian dialogue between the officer and the professor, said, "I assure you, Professor, I really am Leonardo da Vinci returned to a second life. I am grateful for an opportunity to seek your help."

"Well, then," began Professor Montebello, looking at the three teenagers and Leonardo standing crowded in his office, "why don't we—"

Before he could finish his sentence, there was a new knock on the door.

"Now what?" said the professor, speaking Italian. "Yes, come in."

Tad, Gina, and Max all gasped at the same time as Dr. Kastleboro and Ms. Willoughby filled the doorway.

There followed an explosion of conversation, all at the same time, and in a mixture of languages.

"Who are you two?" asked the professor.

"We are the teachers and chaperones for these three students who were missing. We've come to collect them," stated Dr. Kastleboro, responding in Italian.

"What were you three doing running around Florence in a golf cart? And whose cart is it?" asked Ms. Willoughby, addressing the students.

"Nice to see you again," said Leonardo. "Your wonderful students arranged to bring me to this university for a meeting with this professor. Now I feel better about being able to reach my goal."

Tad said, "We thought this is what you would have wanted us to do—be helpful to the most important man in the Renaissance."

Since all of these statements were made at the same time with everybody crowded together in Professor Montebello's small office, nobody understood what was being said.

"Stop! Listen!" shouted Dr. Kastleboro in English, bringing the room to silence. All eyes turned toward the teacher. "You three have caused us a great deal of concern, running all around this city without our knowledge or permission. So we are now going to bundle into a taxi back to the hotel, and I'm shipping you kids home. I will not put up with this conduct. I'm surprised and disappointed in the three of you. It's not what I would have expected."

Tad spoke up, "But, Dr. Kastleboro, we were only… "

"We're leaving now," demanded Dr. Kastleboro.

Ms. Willoughby tried to calm them, saying, "We'll hear your story at the hotel."

Bewildered at the situation, Professor Montebello piped up, "What is all this? Has the kindness of these students created a problem? Fixing problems, I can do."

The teachers turned to the professor. "Yes," spoke Ms. Willoughby in a calmer voice. "Why are these children here? How do you know them?"

Dr. Kastleboro added, "Ms. Willoughby and I are teachers from America. These three students are our charges during this trip to Florence. They are not supposed to be running around Florence without our supervision."

Professor Montebello gasped. "Oh my. I hope I haven't caused any problems for you. These students of yours have been most helpful by giving me a chance to converse with the brilliant and famous Leonardo da Vinci."

The professor waved his hand toward the Maestro, who, while not understanding the exchange in English, watched the conflict unfold.

"But how do you know my three students?" continued Dr. Kastleboro.

Tad, stepped behind the two teachers and looked past them toward the professor, waving his hands and shaking his head in an effort to silence him. But this was to no avail.

Dr. Montebello smiled, not seeing Tad's motions. "I would say we saved each other's lives at the airport."

"Airport?" asked Dr. Kastleboro.

"Why, yes. The news had the story about a man claiming to be the great Leonardo da Vinci and that he was expected to be at the airport for an airplane ride. As a Renaissance scholar, I quickly drove to the airport to get a chance to see this person. My car gave me a misfortune and failed, leaving me stranded. Then I met these three fine young people who happened to also be stranded."

"Stranded?"

"So," continued the professor as Gina, Max and Tad, bracing for the approaching disaster, tried to make themselves as small as possible, "they fixed my car, and I gave them a ride back to Florence. They told me they knew Mr. da Vinci and that he wished to meet a college professor, which I found to be a lucky coincidence because I am a college professor. They then promised that if I loaned them a golf cart, they would find Mr. da Vinci and bring him to me here at the university. And that is what they did. A promise made and a promise kept is to be given praise. They should be commended."

Everyone turned to look at Leonardo, who watched patiently but was puzzled by the conversation he could not understand.

"I think *condemned* is more likely," Gina whispered to Tad.

"Wait," said Ms. Willoughby. "What airplane ride?"

"It was all over the local television. The famous Leonardo da Vinci returned to life and was given an airplane ride to fulfill his dream of flight. These kids made it possible. They took him for his first flight," said the professor.

"Oh, my goodness," exclaimed Ms. Willoughby, turning to glare at the three teenagers. She was instantly grateful that they were on the ground, safe and sound.

Dr. Kastleboro shook his head. "We'll deal with all of this back at the hotel."

Turning to the professor, he said, "Now, did you say you wanted to meet this actor because you believe he really is Leonardo da Vinci, returned from the dead?"

"No, no," Professor Montebello laughed. "But I felt that if this gentleman is truly a reincarnated Leonardo da Vinci, I'd be honored to mentor his introduction to this century. And if he is an actor pretending to be the great genius, which I believe is the case, I plan to play the fool until I can reveal the truth."

Dr. Kastleboro sighed in relief. "Okay then. It's now your play. I am sure that you are far more competent to peel the skin from this onion than I."

Before leaving, Dr. Kastleboro paused, removed a small pad from his pocket and scribbled on a slip of paper before handing it to the professor. "This is my name and address. I would be much obliged if you would drop me a note with the results of your inquiry." Turning to Leonardo he said, "I will now return your 16th century gold florins, all except one which I am keeping to cover my purchase of your 21st century clothing."

Dr. Kastleboro dropped the florins in Leonardo's hands before turning to Gina, Tad, and Max. "Now, you three, that neatly closes our relationship with Mr. da Vinci, which I regret ever began. We are all leaving. Now."

Max whispered to Gina, "Yeah, we are so out of here."

"We'll let the professor sort this out. Come now," said Dr. Kastleboro as he guided them to the door of the office.

"No, wait," Max blurted out. "We must tell the Maestro to focus on energy."

Dr. Kastleboro pulled Max back, saying gruffly, "Come now, Max. The professor will handle it."

Max pulled away, pleading, "No, no. We may only be middle schoolers, but we also have ideas of where we think our future could be."

Max turned to Gina. "Please, Gina, just tell him to work on photosynthesis. Artificial photosynthesis is his best bet."

"Max, what are you talking about?" asked Dr. Kastleboro, while he and Ms. Willoughby attempted to shove and shoo them out.

Gina repeated the translation of Max's suggestion to Leonardo just before she was pulled out of the door.

While Professor Montebello eyed the gold florins in Leonardo's hands with fascination, Leonardo bowed and shook the hands of each teenager before they left, saying, "*Grazie,*" to each one.

The last thing he said before they left was, "I will see you back at the piazza tomorrow morning and tell you of my progress. I feel I need to be there to pursue my quest."

Once they were all gone, Professor Montebello, anxious to get a close look at the gold coins, asked, *"Mi scusi, Maestro, posso vedere quei fiorini?"*

"Si, naturalmente," replied Leonardo, pouring the coins into his palm.

The professor studied the shiny gold coins, tested their heft and nodded. "These look real, but to be five centuries old, and in mint condition, is a contradiction to me."

"Oh, yes, Professor. They're real," said Leonardo.

Professor Montebello then gestured toward a door at the back of the office and said, "Please, Maestro, let's go into my conference room where we will be more comfortable. I need to ask some questions. Then, after a chat, I can show you more of the 21st century."

"This is the moment I've been hoping for, Professor." Leonardo smiled.

He followed the professor into the conference room, where they seated themselves around a table crowded and piled with a myriad of books, papers, and, unbelievably, even more unopened letters.

Leonardo asked, "What did the young man mean by artificial photosynthesis?"

"Oh, I'll try to explain that later," the professor waved his hand absent-mindedly as if shooing away the question. "Before we begin, I must ask you some questions of my own."

"I already know what you will ask," said Leonardo, leaning back in his chair. "I really am Leonardo da Vinci. It is obviously a problem for the citizens of this modern world. Please try to understand.

"My birth in the 15th century was a mistake. I am not bragging, but I was born with a remarkable intelligence that was wasted in those earlier centuries. So, by powers I do not understand, I have been granted a second chance. I must now use the talents given to me to discover or invent something for the betterment of mankind."

As he spoke, the professor began to feel something special simply by being in his presence. Still, he had his own reputation to protect. He could not allow himself to become an unwitting contributor to a colossal hoax if it was one. He needed to be cautious, and remember that, most importantly, dead people do not return to life.

Professor Montebello cleared his throat and continued his task of uncovering whether or not Leonardo was an actor.

"Before we begin to discuss energy and photosynthesis, and before I learn more about these gold florins, pray tell me," he paused, "did you get any of your ideas from the *Nung Shu*?"

Leonardo leaned forward in surprise. "Of course. I never

saw the book, but it was a wonderful source of information. It was brought to Florence by ambassadors from that Oriental empire far to the East."

Shocked at his quick and unhesitating response, the professor asked, "What did you know about the visit?"

"When I was a boy, I learned that a great flotilla of large, square-rigged ships from China sailed to our shores eighteen years before I was born. When they arrived, they carried a book of great knowledge, the *Nung Shu*. That remarkable book offered many innovations and inspired many of my ideas."

"Then, were some of the notes in your notebooks actually ideas from the *Nung Shu*?"

"Some were, most were not. The notebooks were mine, and I added my own ideas and observations, from whatever source."

The professor had studied the history of *Nung Shu*.

The book was not normally connected with Leonardo da Vinci. *Nung Shu* was a book that was carried from China to Venice and Florence by Chinese ambassadors. The ambassadors sailed with the great Chinese merchant fleet under the command of Admiral Zheng He, who with Wang Jinghon, were sent by the Emperor of China, Zhu Zhanji, to visit countries around the world. When the ambassadors arrived in Florence in 1434, they were greeted by Pope Eugenius IV. Gifts of maps, books, and other treasures of knowledge were presented to the officials of Florence and to the pope.

In organizing the vast armada of a thousand ships, it was the plan of Emperor Zhu Zhanji to establish trade with nations far from China. He was particularly interested in those countries he considered to be inhabited by barbarians. Florence was one of the places he understood to be an important city among the barbarian people in the western culture. He considered them barbarians because they were constantly at war with one another. The emperor thought that conquering by fighting and killing was wrong. Living in peace, exchanging knowledge and buying and selling goods was, in his opinion, a far more effective way for countries to treat and deal with each other.

At that time, China was far more advanced in the sciences, medicine, and technology than the countries of Europe. The fleet was sent by the emperor on its journey to spread and gain knowledge and create trade. He believed that sending his fleet to all parts of the world would accomplish this peaceful purpose while also uniting other countries under the influence of China, quietly and without force.

Unfortunately, when he died, the new emperor acted on his own barbaric ideas. He disbanded the fleet and used the gained wealth to create an army to attack the Mongolian people to the north of China. In the attempt, he lost, and the fleet of good will was then lost to the world.

When Professor Montebello studied the codices of Leonardo da Vinci, he formed a belief that some of the ideas that appeared in the notebooks were ideas from that Chinese book. He was surprised that this actor actually knew of *Nung Shu*.

At the spot where Leonardo was seated, a handful of paper clips had spilled onto the table. While the professor was talking, Leonardo fidgeted with them as if trying to figure out what their purpose was. After a few minutes, he began to assemble them in a chain. When his chain was almost two feet long he pulled on it to test its strength.

Leonardo then realized that the professor was watching him.

He held up the chain and said, "This chain is very weak. What are these links for? Is this for a lady's necklace?"

Professor Montebello said, "Not particularly pretty as a lady's necklace. Here, I'll show you." Lifting two pieces of paper from the table, he clipped them together with a paper clip.

Leonardo watched in fascination. Then he nodded and mimicked the professor by clipping several pieces of paper together. "Very clever," he said.

The professor cocked his head to one side, wondering how he could trap the man into revealing if he was an actor. He said, "Of course, if you are indeed the man himself, then I'd be remiss if I didn't ask you this question. What is the real story as to why in 1478 the Pazzi plot to assassinate Lorenzo and Giuliano de Medici failed? The men behind the assassination were to take control of the banking business and the leadership of Florence. So, why didn't it work? Did the Duomo as

Florence's premier cathedral and most sacred church have anything to do with the failure? Was the failure religious?"

Without pause, Leonardo said, "Yes, I think so. Giovanni Battista, the Count of Montesecco, who had military skills, was the designated assassin. When the location planned for the assassination changed from a dinner party to inside the cathedral, he refused to commit the murder since it was in a holy building. In his place, two others, Bernardo Baroncelli and Francesco di Pazzi, accepted the assignment to murder the two brothers. These two men had no experience in this type of business at all and, of course, they botched the job. They ended up killing only Giuliano and not Lorenzo. I even remember making a sketch in my codex of the hanging of Baroncelli."

Leonardo paused and stroked his beard thoughtfully. "I appreciate your need to determine if I am really Leonardo da Vinci or just a person pretending to be me. That's perfectly logical. And I am glad to answer all of your questions, but I have things I need to see and learn."

"Of course," said Professor Montebello. "What can I do?"

"Could I see one of those devices I heard of called a microscope?"

"Yes, absolutely. That is easy." The professor rose from his seat, opened a nearby door and led Leonardo along a hall and up a flight of stairs. At the top of the stairs, they turned into a short alcove and entered a laboratory. The room was filled with glass-fronted cabinets, which in turn were cluttered with glass beakers, test tubes, funnels, volumetric flasks, and jars containing powders of assorted colors. Around the room were sinks next to counters containing Bunsen burners, microscopes, and jars of mysterious liquids. The entire laboratory smelled like vinegar mixed with an unknown sulfuric compound.

"Why don't you sit here, Maestro," the professor suggested as he lifted a gray protective cloth from a microscope. "Now look through the eyepieces on this scope and twist the knob up and down with your hand until the picture you see is clear. First, I am going to put on several slides of plant and animal cells."

As Leonardo looked through the glass, he was amazed at what he saw. Leonardo remained at the microscope for half an hour as the professor changed slides, varying between human, animal and plant samples.

Finally, Leonardo exclaimed, "Amazing. Complicated. Overwhelming."

"Now, some fun," chuckled Professor Montebello as he placed a new blank slide under the scope. He added a drop of water that was standing on the counter, knowing it would be teeming with bacteria.

This time when Leonardo looked into the microscope, he did not dare take his eyes away from the scope as bacteria squirmed before him. The tiny creatures wriggled and twisted across the slide. "*Incredibile! Magico!*" was all Leonardo could muster.

Leonardo asked, "Did you say these are bacteria?"

"Why, yes."

"There are bacteria in the water we drink?" He scrunched up his nose in disgust.

"Of course."

Leonardo gasped, "Then wouldn't anyone who drinks this kind of water become ill from bacteria?"

"Why do you ask that?"

Thinking back to his conversation with the students, Leonardo said, "I was told that bacteria caused diseases."

"Well, yes and no. It's not that simple. If you wish, I can try to explain. But for now just notice the different bacteria as I put on different slides."

"I do want to see," said Leonardo. "but first, do you think this is an area where I might be able to direct my quest?"

"Oh, I don't know. It depends upon what you already know about medicine. For instance, what vaccinations have you had?" Here, the professor hoped to catch Leonardo make a mistake by revealing that he knew what a vaccination was.

"I don't understand," Leonardo replied blankly.

"Well," Professor Montebello trailed off. He paused, realizing how every statement Leonardo made remained consistent with a person ignorant of the 21st century. Professor Montebello looked away, frowning. He wondered if this Leonardo da Vinci actor may not be an actor at all. *It just might be true,* he thought. He shook his head, affirming to himself that if this were a farce, he would become the laughing stock of the university. He needed a plan to really find out the truth.

Turning to Leonardo, he rubbed his hands together excitedly and then extended them outward as if about to embrace him. Beaming, Professor Montebello said, "Why don't you take your time with the microscope while I locate other professors with whom you may wish to raise your questions? We can all talk more this afternoon. Afterwards, you'll be my guest for dinner and I can answer more questions and you can do the same for me."

Still hunched over the microscope, riveted by the bacteria, Leonardo mumbled, "Yes, that would be most kind. Oh! But please before you go," he jumped up excitedly, "please explain to me what the young students meant by photosynthesis?"

Surprised, Professor Montebello stammered, "Well, yes, alright."

The professor cleared his throat and explained, "It is an extremely complex process. Light rays from the sun are absorbed in plants through food-making cells called chloroplasts. These cells contain chlorophyll. In these cells, the atoms in the water drawn from the soil are split into their hydrogen and oxygen parts. The hydrogen is combined with carbon dioxide from the air to form food-creating substances. It uses other chemicals such as nitrogen, sulfur, or phosphorus to make the basics of food, and the oxygen is released into the air we breathe. Through this process, plants not only clean the air, but create energy. The rays of the sun are absorbed by plants and turned into food and oxygen—that is the basic function of the process known as photosynthesis.

"To put it simply, the sun gives energy to the plants, animals and humans eat the plants, and animals and humans eat the animals that eat the plants. That is the manner in which energy from the sun is distributed. Plants provide further methods of energy production through the burning of wood, coal, or oil or even products made from them. The circle of life depends on the sun.

"In fact, the Earth receives more energy in one hour from the sun than the whole world uses in a year. Some believe it is to the sun that humankind must look for the future of clean energy. They see it as an energy source without limit."

He added, "That young friend of yours was suggesting that you invent artificial photosynthesis, where energy from the sun is converted to electricity directly through the plant leaves. The direct energy conversion idea is imaginary and does not exist. No such thing."

Leonardo replied slowly, "I'm having trouble grasping this new concept. Perhaps you could spend more time explaining it to me."

The professor nodded his head, chuckling softly. "A strange topic for a beginning conversation, but I'll do my best." He smiled. "We have much to share, much to talk about."

Shuffling slowly out of the room, Professor Montebello said, "Now, I think I'll go and invite a few colleagues as I suggested before, a gathering of learned men to advise and educate you."

"Most kind of you," Leonardo muttered as he turned back excitedly to look at the microscope once more.

"You relax here," directed the professor. "I'll be back shortly."

While he waited, Leonardo reflected upon the astonishing revelations he had seen through the eyepiece of the microscope. *The mysteries of nature revealed through the device seemed so commonplace to the professor and even to his young friends. I'm anxious to be introduced to men of great learning, but am I capable of embracing five centuries of new discoveries in one evening? I was vastly more intelligent than other men of my time, but am I more intelligent than the men of this modern world?*

I fear that I will never accomplish my quest as a middle-aged man with my limited 16th century experience. It won't work. I needed to have started younger, to attend to a 21st century school and learn the basics of contemporary mathematics, science, and history. I needed to begin at the same age as before—when my father apprenticed me to the studios of

Andrea del Verrocchio. I might even need to know a new language.

What if appearing in Florence as an older man has doomed me to never accomplish anything significant in the short amount of time I have? What if the do-over was fun, but a mistake... yet another mistake?

ঃ০০ঃ

Once in the hall, Professor Montebello hurried to the faculty lounge, where he found three of his friends surrounding some chess players.

"Gentlemen," he said, "I have an afternoon and evening that I guarantee will be far more exciting than a chess match."

"What is that?" asked one of the men.

"Leonardo da Vinci," he said.

There was a pause. Then one of the men asked, "What about him?"

"He's in my laboratory, and I thought some of you would like to join the conversation."

"You mean that guy that's been all over the television and radio, mocking our mayor?"

"The very one."

"How did you pull that off?"

"Three children brought him to me to teach him modern science. He claims he was reincarnated to help the world with his genius."

One of the professors smirked. "I'm sure the world will be grateful." They all laughed.

The other chess player asked, "Why are you entertaining this man?"

Professor Montebello chimed, "Because, gentlemen, it seems like a very good idea. As a look-alike, he's almost perfect, and as a Renaissance scholar, he's impressive. He actually wants me to teach him the basic science of plant photosynthesis of all things."

One man sighed and rolled his eyes. "But why are you even bothering with this man?"

"Because I don't know what his game is. My suspicion is that he is one of those famous Hollywood stars, pulling a stunt to stir interest in some new movie. You know, create buzz while enjoying free press. Maybe we, as a group, might be able to reach the truth about his real identity and understand this whole charade."

The men looked at each other and, shrugging, rose to join Professor Montebello. As they approached the laboratory, there was a clatter that echoed along the corridors in the opposite direction. In a moment, it became clear. The noise was from Antonio Gigliardi, his camera man and a handful of other television and newspaper reporters.

As the two parties met halfway down a long hallway, Gigliardi bellowed, "Do any of you gentlemen know where Professor Montebello's office is?"

"Yes, I know, because I am Professor Montebello."

"Great." Gigliardi grinned. "We're looking for this Leonardo da Vinci look-alike. He darted away from a great gathering with a bunch of kids in a golf cart, and according to my police friend, he was heading here."

"Well, he is here," said Professor Montebello, "but I don't think he wants anything to do with television."

"Great. Great," said Gigliardi, "He's an entertainment genius. Puts on a great performance in front of national, even international TV, then has a gimmick exit."

"Gimmick?"

"You betcha." Gigliardi's camera man smirked. "Three kids in a golf cart darting through the piazza out toward the Duomo? Kooky. Great TV."

"And I've got a great time slot for him," added Gigliardi.

Professor Montebello shrugged. "In that case, you must ask him yourself. I, for one, would love to see his reaction. Here, right down the hall, he's in the lab."

At the laboratory, the group opened the door, found it dark and noticed the shades were drawn.

"Ah, *Signore Leonardo*," said Professor Montebello, "I'm sorry. I seem to have left you in the dark. I forgot to show you how to turn on a light switch."

He reached for the switch and flipped on the light. The fluorescence filled the room. The professors and the media all stood in the doorway... shocked.

Leonardo da Vinci was gone.

13. BACK HOME

When the teachers and the students gathered back in the lobby of the hotel, Max, Gina, and Tad remained silent.

Dr. Kastleboro paced in front of them, not taking his eyes off of them for an instant. Ms. Howdershell stood nearby with her arms crossed, her usually easy-going expression now tense and stern.

Dr. Kastleboro grumbled, "I am aware that you three were speeding through Florence in a borrowed golf cart. I understand that it was not a joy ride, but for the specific purpose of accommodating the Leonardo da Vinci look-alike. What is not clear to me is why you were at the airport?"

Ms. Willoughby shook her head. "Did you actually ride in an airplane with that stranger?"

None of the three answered. Gina and Max looked at Tad. Tad, in turn, looked at the formidable wall of angry teachers as he searched his brain for the right answer. At that moment, he remembered the advice from his grandfather, a rough mountain man from the backwoods of the Appalachian Mountains, "I'll tell you, boy," his grandfather had said, "When all else fails, try the truth."

Tad told the teachers the story of the plan and the airplane ride, leaving out the part about the tailspin. Finally, he added, "But, Dr. Kastleboro, you are the one who invited him to meet us."

"That's true," Dr. Kastleboro said, wrinkling his brow in disapproval. "I know that I brought this actor into our trip. Still," he growled, "taking an airplane ride without adult permission, or any supervision at all, is not acceptable. Way out of bounds, and I think all of you knew that without being told. As far as I am concerned, I am ready to put you three on a non-stop plane for home."

"Whoa," Ms. Howdershell spoke. "Not so fast. I think the first thing we need to do is to contact the principal and get her take on this."

Dr. Kastleboro stopped pacing. For a moment he was quiet. Then, finally, he said, "It's six hours earlier where she is. This would be a good time to call."

He pointed sternly to the students, "You three will not move, understand?"

No one spoke as he left for the phone booth.

With the conversation over, Ms. Willoughby excused herself to get back to the other students.

Alone with Ms. Howdershell peering at them through disappointed eyes, the students looked at each other nervously.

Tad gripped his hands into fists to try to stop himself from shaking and giving away how nervous he was. He couldn't stand up to Dr. Kastleboro, but he could stand up for his friends and for their goal of helping Leonardo. Despite his fear of what the consequences would be, he was ready and willing to accept them.

Max grew dizzy as he tried to think of different strategies to save them. Adding up the strategies, he came up with zero plausible ones. His head began to ache at the thought of there being no solution to their problem.

Gina blinked back tears as she nibbled on her lip, fearing what her parents might say when they found out she, and her friends, broke the rules.

As they shared eye contact simultaneously, they all agreed on one thing—it was worth it.

Soon enough, Dr. Kastleboro returned. "Well," he sighed, "The principal said you all can stay and return with the group as scheduled. She will notify each of your parents and set up a meeting with them when you return. In the meantime, you all are placed in the personal charge of Ms. Howdershell."

Gina, Max, and Tad all exchanged looks of temporary relief. Whatever doom awaited them would at least wait, even if only temporarily.

Ms. Howdershell gestured to the students, beckoning them to come close to her. "You three will stick close to me, and I mean extremely close. Expect an extra busy next two days. Together, we will visit the Duomo, the Uffizi Art Gallery, the Galleria della Accademia, the Galileo Museum, and a great number of the many art galleries and fine churches here in Florence. I am sure you will all enjoy this cultural education."

Tad couldn't help himself as he blurted out as quickly as he could, "But Ms. Howdershell, we're supposed to meet the Maestro tomorrow morning in the Piazza della Signoria."

Ms. Howdershell grinned. "That's okay. We'll meet him together. I have some serious questions of my own to ask that man."

The next morning, they enjoyed breakfast at one of the open tables beside the Piazza della Signoria, but Leonardo da Vinci did not appear.

For the next two days, Tad, Gina, and Max trailed quietly alongside Ms. Howdershell to every museum and art gallery in Florence that she favored. They also listened to an endless series of ancient art and history lectures.

For their flight home, each was seated separately and next to a teacher. However, when the teachers weren't watching, they would look at each other and smile, sharing the secret of their crazy journey with the one and only Leonardo da Vinci.

They arrived at Dulles Airport on Saturday afternoon. On Sunday morning there was a meeting in a conference room at Longfellow Middle School. The host of the meeting was assistant principal, Mr. Ocampo, and the three teachers, along with Max's mother, Mildred Peabody; Tad's father, John Sullivan, and Gina's parents, Cmdr. Anthony and Norma Brunelli. Everyone else was seated around the table, but Ms. Peabody insisted on standing next to a bookshelf with her arms crossed.

"Well," began Mr. Ocampo, "We seem to have a situation on our hands." He studied his notes which were scribbled on a yellow legal pad. "I understand that you all met a man dressed in a 16th century costume who favored the looks of Leonardo da Vinci. And," he continued, "he claimed to be the original Leonardo da Vinci, reincarnated after 500 years because he was born by accident in the wrong century. Then, in spite of the fact that the teachers all informed you that dead people do not return to life, you all insisted that the Leonardo look-alike was, in fact, the original Renaissance hero restored to life. Ignoring the warning, you all undertook—without permission—to entertain this notion, run off with him, host him in an airplane ride over the Tuscan countryside and taxi him around Florence in a borrowed golf cart."

He paused. "Have I got this right so far?"

The three students nodded.

"And, although he claimed friendship and gratitude for your time and the money you spent on him, he mysteriously disappeared as suddenly as he had appeared, leaving the three of you to face the disappointment and anger of your chaperones, your parents and me." He paused again and looked directly at each of them. "Now tell me, do you still believe what this costumed-man told you or do you now accept the obvious truth?"

Tad looked at the others. Both Gina and Max shook their heads. "I'm sorry, Sir, but we believe he was… he is… really real—really Leonardo da Vinci."

Mr. Ocampo was astonished. "You three exercised bad judgment in Florence and continue to exercise bad judgment now. Let me be very direct. Dead people stay dead."

"But…" Max began.

"Finally," continued the assistant principal, waving Max to be quiet, "your friend, Neville Klaxton, unearthed your airplane plan, but out of a sense of loyalty, he kept silent. He should have reported your dangerous antics immediately to one of the teachers." Then he added as an aside, "You should be proud to have such a loyal friend."

The three looked at each other, but made no response.

He continued, "I don't think I need to tell you what you did was wrong. You should have described your plans to the teachers and let them guide your conduct. I can tell you, from the point of view of the administration, we are all tremendously relieved that no harm has come to any one of you. I can also say that we are most disappointed in your actions." He turned to Dr. Kastleboro, "Do you have anything you wish to add?"

Dr. Kastleboro rose from his chair.

"No," said Mr. Ocampo, "keep your seat. This is an informal inquiry."

"He means, inquest," whispered Gina to Max.

Dr. Kastleboro said, "I do regret bringing this costumed man into our trip, but at the time I thought it would make an exciting adventure. I still have one of the gold florins which I will take to Capitol Coin & Stamp on 17th Street downtown for authentication. But it is obvious that I never would have approved of an airplane flight. Never."

Tad's father frowned as he listened. Then he asked, "Do you think there was any educational value from this adventure?"

"Probably," answered, Dr. Kastleboro. "We certainly learned that we all need to be careful of strangers. The Leonardo impersonator was extremely pleasant and friendly, probably a con man, because there is no such thing as an unpleasant con man. The lesson here is that a con man will always make you want to like him and to trust him—otherwise he could not cheat or fool you."

Max responded, "But, Dr. Kastleboro, he didn't cheat us."

"True enough, Max," said Dr. Kastleboro, "but he did fool you."

"Unless, of course, he really was Leonardo da Vinci, reincarnated," quipped Mr. Sullivan without changing his frown. After a pause, he turned to Mr. Ocampo and said, "I know you intend to punish the kids for their behavior. But if you don't mind, I believe I know the appropriate punishment for my son. I trust you will allow me to administer the proper punishment at home."

Mr. Ocampo was surprised, but in a greater sense, pleased, not to have to come up with a fitting punishment. "I think I've got this covered," continued Mr. Sullivan. "Come on, son, I'll deal with you at home."

Mrs. Peabody, from her standing position by the bookshelves, scowled, "I've heard enough. I agree with Mr. Sullivan. I think these impressionable kids were put in a position to believe this fairytale. They think they're grownups dealing with grownup problems, but they're not. Not many years ago they were still putting quarters under their pillows for the tooth fairy, for goodness sake.

"I don't need this meeting." she said, going over to Max. "I'll deal with him at home. And don't you worry, Mr. Ocampo, he'll not be fooled like this again."

When they had gone, only Gina and her parents were left behind. No one spoke for a while, and then Mrs. Brunelli broke the silence. "If I understand this meeting, we're here to discuss the conduct of our children mostly about sneaking away from their chaperones and taking a secret and dangerous airplane flight?"

"In a nutshell, yes," agreed Mr. Ocampo.

"Well then," said Mrs. Brunelli, "Gina, did not get in that airplane. She was simply with the two boys who did. I'm grateful that she had the good sense to say no to this flight."Then she added, as she rose to leave, "Thank you for hosting this meeting. I look forward to learning if this da Vinci look-alike character ever reappears—which, of course, will not happen. He was probably some Italian publicity stunt."

"One that worked," added her husband.

With that, Gina followed her father and mother out of the room.

"Well," said Mr. Ocampo, "that's not what I expected, but I guess things have been resolved satisfactorily." Then turning to the three teachers, "Was the actor really that good?"

"Really good," Dr. Kastleboro replied, shaking his head. "He was so good, there were times when I believed he really was *the* Leonard da Vinci, but then reality would kick in. It was quite uncanny."

℘ℛ

In the car, Tad was direct with his father. "Am I in big trouble, Dad?"

"Absolutely," said his father, hiding a smile. "For the next six months, your driving privileges are revoked."

Tad regarded his father with a puzzled look. "But, Dad, I'm too young, I don't have a driver's license."

His father nodded. "Hmm," he said, still suppressing a smile as he made a left-hand turn, "I'm not negotiating. Six months. Deal with it."

℘ℛ

When Max and his mother were alone, she asked, "Max, tell me, did you really think this guy was the great Leonardo da Vinci reincarnated?"

"Yes, Mom, I did and I still do."

"You know, Max, reincarnation does not happen."

"Except this time, Mom. He was real. I just know it..."

His mother shrugged her shoulders and said, "Please don't go around announcing that you believe such nonsense. I'm just glad I didn't know what you were doing when you were doing it. That was dangerous. You were foolish. Being foolish is not like you. That airplane could have crashed." She held her son in front of her with her hands on his shoulders. "We're so glad

161

you're home safe and sound. Please don't do dangerous things like that again."

"Yes, Mama," he replied. "My bad."

ℴℴ

Gina and her parents drove to a café to grab a bite to eat. "Frankly, dear," her mother began, "as nutty as it was for you three kids to run off and charter an aircraft for the stranger, I'm glad that you exercised good judgment by not actually getting into that craft."

"Well, mom, I did help set it up," confessed Gina.

"Yes, honey, but you didn't actually get into the airplane. Intentions are different than actions."

ℴℴ

The next day, the cafeteria was noisy as usual when the three friends finally met again for their first lunch together back at school. Word had already circulated through their class that Max, Gina, and Tad claimed to have met the famous Leonardo da Vinci, reincarnated, and traveled with this stranger in a forbidden airplane ride. It was rumored that they really believed that the hero of the Renaissance had been blessed with a do-over, as an opportunity to live in the 21st century, and had come back from the dead, becoming their close personal friend. The story became a school joke.

"If Tad is Leonardo and Gina is Vinci, who do you think is Da?" was Neville's oft-repeated jest. "Must be Max."

Since their three teachers acknowledged that the Leonardo da Vinci reenactor was remarkably talented, the class concluded that Max, Gina, and Tad had been made into fools for believing he was real. After all, it was Florence and tourism was their big industry—why wouldn't there be a reenactor?

No one knew where he had come from or where he went when he disappeared, and no one had a phone number or an address. After Max, Tad and Gina left Leonardo at the University to meet with the professor, they never heard from him again.

Meanwhile, throughout Florence, in the newspapers and on the television news, the talk was about the man who had appeared with the mayor claiming to be Leonardo da Vinci. His singing of the *Dies Irae* was given rave reviews. Experts agreed that the hastily drawn sketches the man had made were very Leonardo da Vincian (whatever that meant), but were of an inferior quality.

The three American teachers also agreed that the man, who-ever he was, was a talented artist, and certainly a charming person. They pointed out that whatever his motive, he stirred attention, but they admitted that his "end game" was not clear. Probably, hopefully, one day they would learn. Maybe someday he would appear in a role in a movie or a musical show on Broadway or on television. They were sure that when he did, they would recognize him.

Neville, not one to pass up an opportunity, teased them constantly, saying, "Only our three idiot classmates who believe in ghosts were fooled."

Later, as the three sat at their favorite cafeteria table, several of the girls in their class passed by and asked if they would like to come over to sit at the table with Neville and his friends. The girls didn't wait for the answer. They just giggled and walked away.

"Well," said Gina, "do you guys think we were fools after all?"

"No," said Tad.

Max confessed, "Absolutely not. I think we failed him because we believed in him, but didn't really help him."

Gina frowned, asking, "But why was it our responsibility to help him? Shouldn't the leaders and scholars in Florence have been the ones to assist?"

Max sighed, "Probably, but I still feel bad because we undertook the task, but didn't succeed." He sighed, adding, "I, for one, hate failure."

Tad elbowed him jokingly, "I'll bet not as much as the Maestro."

Ignoring the exchange, Gina wondered aloud, "I wonder where he went."

Max guessed, "It may have been exactly what he said. If he did not use his special intelligence to make a new discovery or create a new invention, his do-over would end."

Tad gasped, "You mean he died all over again?"

"Yeah. Returned to his grave."

As Tad's face tensed in remorse, Gina patted him on the back and said, "Look, there's not much we can do here at Longfellow. We'll be the butt of jokes for a while, but then the semester will be over. Next fall we'll be in high school, and all of this will be forgotten."

ᔓᲝᲚ

Television stories circulated on the networks all throughout the summer. Reporters seemed to refuse to drop "the return of Leonardo da Vinci" stories. First, there was the report leaked to CNN that Interpol was unable to track the fingerprint of the Leonardo da Vinci impersonator lifted from a wine glass. The mayor later announced, "Interpol searched their database and those from most of the participating countries, but the man claiming to be Leonardo da Vinci has no police record, no court records, and no passport." He added, "There was no trace of any school record, military record, or job record—nothing!"

A man who could sing a Gregorian Chant in both tenor and baritone, while holding a microphone in his right hand and drawing clever cartoons with his left was indeed a talent worth tracking. In spite of that, no one could recall seeing him leave Florence on any form of public transportation, and there was no car registered to him.

As a result of the media on the events in Florence, Bruno Manetti, a wealthy businessman in Rome, offered to cover the cost of employing a private investigator to go to Seattle, in the United States, and negotiate with the billionaire, Bill Gates, for permission to dust for fingerprints on two or three of the pages of an original Leonardo notebook called the Leicester Codex. This was the famous da Vinci codex that Bill Gates had purchased for his private collection.

The remarkable thing about the investigation was that while there were literally hundreds of fingerprints found around the edges of the pages of the codex and even though most of the fingerprints had faded into the fuzzy antiquity of hundreds of years, three suspected points of an index print were found that matched the Leonardo da Vinci impersonator's.

While various experts weighed in with lengthy television and newspaper commentary about the three points, the final conclusion was that the data were too weak to support any reasonable conclusion.

Max, Gina, and Tad felt vindicated when they read the story of the fingerprints in *The Washington Post*, but no one paid any attention to them. It was yesterday's news.

A week or two into the new school season at Langley High School, the principal addressed the freshman class and announced a new mentor program.

"You are now the proud members of the class of 2004. Think of our times. One hundred years ago, we were a nation of farmers. Our interstate road system did not exist. Transportation was horses, oxen, bicycles, trains, and steam boats. We were a very insular people. Foreigners were fleeing their countries to seek refuge at our shores, but few Americans ever had an opportunity to see people from these countries except in self-segregated communities. Things have changed tremendously in this last century. We, here at Langley today, are lucky because we have a community of very fine and diverse students from all over the world.

"Some in our community are new to our school. Some are new to America. For that reason, I am excited to tell you about our new mentor program. For this program, I am soliciting help from each of the new freshmen of Langley High to find those students just beginning at Longfellow Middle School and mentor and guide these students on their way into our country, our community, and our wonderful school system."

He paused and scanned the auditorium pointedly. "I look forward to a large turnout for this new opportunity."

After polite applause, the principal left and several teachers shuffled amongst the students in search for volunteers.

Max, Tad, and Gina put their heads together and then asked one of the teachers if they could help as a team.

Max spoke for the group, saying, "We believe that we could better serve as a team. Together, we are more effective, with each of us helping in different ways."

The teacher agreed, and the next day, their homeroom teacher sent them over to Longfellow Middle School to meet their mentee.

As they entered the seventh grade homeroom class, the three agreed that Tad would make their pitch.

Tad announced, "Listen up, I am Tad Sullivan. With me are Gina Brunelli and Max Peabody. We're now in high school, but we've been where you are now, and as a team we will be here to help with your transition into your new life in middle school. If you want our help, just come on over and introduce yourself."

It was then that a voice, strange in pitch and yet familiar in tone, said, "You three will be perfect to help me."

They looked around and in unison said, "Maestro! It's you!"

Walking toward them, he responded in a whisper with accented English, "No more Leonardo da Vinci. I am back, but I am now Leonard Vinciti."

"What? How? What happened?" Gina asked question after question, while the boys stared with eyes as wide as saucers.

"At the University, I waited in the laboratory while Professor Montebello left to bring some of his friends. I was fascinated with what I was seeing in the microscope. Then I began to wonder how much they could really teach me during the course of an afternoon and a dinner. I knew that the professor did not believe I was returned from the 16th century and that he was testing me. I felt he was mocking me the whole time."

He continued, "It occurred to me that I was already a middle-aged man, too old to advance five hundred years so suddenly.

"Whatever power had rescued me from the error of my original birth in the wrong century must have understood my dilemma. In Florence, I returned to the 21st century in the wrong place at the wrong age of my life. That error has now been corrected. I am now here in middle school, in America, speaking English, and, best of all, I have my three noble friends to help me."

Tad asked, "How did you do that?"

"You mean how did I travel?"

"Yes, how did you travel back in age and all the way to America?"

"I took a bus."

"A bus?"

He chuckled. "Just kidding. I traveled the same mysterious way. In a whirlwind cloud through a prism." Placing his hand on Tad's shoulder, he said, "Listen, the most important thing is that Max was right. Max identified the perfect project for me—artificial photosynthesis. When I realized how right he was, I knew it was beyond anything that Professor Montebello or any of the other university professors could teach me. I realized that I was still a 16th century person with a 16th century vision of life. I realized that I could never understand photosynthesis at the sophisticated level needed to artificially create the majesty of nature's product.

"At the very moment that I had that realization, I was suddenly transported through time and age to here and now. There is more that I cannot explain. All I can say is that I am here now with the opportunity to become sufficiently educated, so that I can attempt to invent artificial photosynthesis. I need to honor my newly granted second opportunity for a do-over."

Gina asked Max, "I don't remember. Why artificial photosynthesis?"

"Easy," Max answered. "The logic is very straightforward. All energy on the Earth comes from the sun. The energy from the sun's rays can give everyone all the power they will ever need. If the energy from the sun can be artificially photosynthesized and utilized on a massive, industrial strength scale, then a worldwide, clean, endless source of energy would revolutionize our world and be a wondrous benefit for all mankind."

Leonard said, "That's the idea. However, in order for me to realistically focus on the problem, I need to have a 21st century education. Your world is now at a level of sophistication that is assembling information and building new devices at ever increasing speeds.

"When I thought about it, I realized that I must not only learn all there is at the middle school and high school level, but I must also engage in university studies, then at advanced levels before I can create this magic—artificial photosynthesis.

"A formal, structured education in this century is absolutely essential to being able to change the future. It is true that you need a window into the past to give you a basis for opening a door to the future, but with the speed of science today, I cannot reach my goal without learning in a depth and detail I could not get alone. So I needed to begin here in middle school."

"But, Leonard," asked Gina, "why here and not Florence?"

"And," said Max, "how come you're not in California where so much of this research takes place?"

Leonard smiled. "Because I also need you three. You believed in me. I trust each of you to help me. I have a lot to learn to just get along in this century, in this community, and in this school. The big studies will come later—university and, then, graduate studies.

"Remember, I am still the same old Leonardo da Vinci. Being a 16th century genius is only good for the 16th century. I need more—I need an education. I am barely out of your elementary schools in formal knowledge. I need your mentor skills, your guidance, your interaction, and your team intellect. I need you all."

"Then we're all on board," said Max, speaking for the three companions.

Everyone in the class was surprised to witness a four-way hug.

"Well, I'll be," said the homeroom teacher. "I've never seen high school kids actually hug a seventh grader. I'll have to watch that Leonard boy. They must know something I don't."

They certainly did.

14. THE FINAL ADVENTURE

Gina Brunelli sat at her desk and stared absently at the cityscape of New York as it spread out below her 70th floor window of the Empire State Building. Her life in New York was exciting and challenging as the Assistant Director of Formidable Media Solutions, an influential media company.

It was 3:30 on a sunny Friday afternoon when an overnight package was delivered to her desk. The return address read the Xylem Robotic Institute in Oakland, California. Inside the package was a white envelope that held a carefully handwritten note. Gina was puzzled. This was the year 2020 and no one sent handwritten notes any more. Flashmail and the recent Tracy were the usual modes of communication.

The note was an invitation to meet with Dr. Li Chow, Vice President of Xylem Robotic Institute, on the following Monday. Inside the Federal Express package was a reservation for a roundtrip passage on the exciting, new, and luxurious Concorde II, a supersonic luxury airplane offering coast-to-coast service.

Her flight was from New York to Oakland. Also in the package were reservations at the Waterfront Hotel, in the newly updated Jack London Square. The note stated that a limousine would meet her at the airport and transport her to the hotel. Finally, the note said that her destination was within easy walking distance of the hotel. Directions to her destination would be at the front desk on her arrival. No further explanation was provided.

Curious, she thought, *Why would the vice president of Xylem Robotic Institute send me a ticket—and why all the secrecy? I'm a marketing person. I know nothing about robots.*

The note was still in her hand when her desk phone buzzed.

"There is a call on line one from a Dr. Harlan Maxfield Peabody," her assistant said when Gina picked up.

"Thank you," Gina answered. As the call went through, she pressed a button and his smiling face appeared on her desktop Facefone III-D screen. "Max," exclaimed Gina, smiling back "How are you?"

"A little fried. I've been grading advanced applied mathematics tests all day. But things are well." Over the years, Max had become the youngest full-tenured professor at the University of California, Berkeley, near Oakland. "I'm happy to take a break. What about you? How are you?"

"The usual. I've been busy," replied Gina. "You know, everything moves fast here in New York."

Max chuckled as he leaned back into his chair while a ReadyBoard slowly erased itself behind him. He must have ended a class just before making the call.

After high school, the friends had drifted apart, but then had reconnected in 2014 at their 10th high school reunion. Since then, they had stayed connected. They particularly enjoyed checking in with each other on the Tracy, the new electronic voice and text wristwatch, named after the imaginary radio watch first created in the newspaper comic strip Dick Tracy by the cartoonist Chester Gould, in January, 1946.

"Did you get a letter from Xylem Robotic Institute and a plane ticket?" asked Max.

"Yes, just now. How did you know?"

"I also received a note. And I contacted Tad."

Tad had served several tours in the Marines and was now living in New Orleans working for a Mississippi barge company. "He also received a mysterious note."

"Okay, Max," said Gina. "Do you know what this is all about?"

"I think so, Gina. It's in the name: Xylem."

"I don't get it. What does Xylem have to do with you, Tad, and me?"

"It's him, Gina. I'm pretty sure, it's him."

"Who?"

"Leonard."

"You mean the long-lost Maestro has reappeared?"

"Yes. The name 'Xylem' is a word in botany. It's the name of the tissue that absorbs water at the bottom of a plant's roots. If over these last decades he has been working on artificial photosynthesis, then he has to be involved with botany. If my guess is right, the name means we found Leonard—or rather, he found, and is sending for, us."

"Well," said Gina, nodding thoughtfully, "I remember that when we all went off to college, he went to M.I.T. and then disappeared from our lives. We all tried, but none of us could find him."

"Now, perhaps he has found us, and if it is him, then I'm sure it's for a purpose."

"What do you mean, 'a purpose,' Max?" Gina asked. Out of habit, she doodled endless circles on the notepad. And soon after, she began writing letters backwards as she subconsciously thought about Leonardo da Vinci.

"I think he must be in trouble. Remember, back in high school, we were always the ones getting him out of trouble." Max continued, "Don't forget, we are the only ones who know who he really is."

"And if we told anybody now, we'd be laughed at more than in those early years," she chuckled.

She paused and watched the face on the screen. "So what's the plan?"

"If he sent you an airline ticket, use it. Give me your flight information and I'll meet you at the Airport."

171

"What about Tad?"

"He'll be here. We'll all gather at the Waterfront Hotel. There will be another note for us at the desk. I'm excited for all of us to be together again." Then he added, "And I'm sure the three of us together will be able to solve whatever mess our long-lost friend has gotten himself into."

"Of course," Gina replied, grinning. She paused as the face on the screen nodded. "I wonder what kind of distress caused him to reach back into his past to call in the troops—if we're considered 'the troops'?"

"Hard to guess, Gina. We should know soon enough," Max told her. "It's also possible that it could be something else entirely, but I think I'm right."

"I would expect nothing less from you, Max." She paused as she watched his expression change from deep thought to a renewed smile. Gina spoke again, "And, if you guessed correctly, it will now be the four of us. It's been a long time." She paused. "I'll be on the Concorde II on Monday."

As soon as she closed the line, she contacted the airline to confirm her flight. Next, she called her boss to arrange for a few personal days away from the office. Finally, she picked up her phone and scheduled a taxi.

ℰℭ

The cab driver noticed Gina's excitement.

"You flying on the new Concorde II?" he guessed.

"Yes. Yes, I am," she responded. "How did you know that?"

"You seem too excited for a seat in economy," he chuckled. "Have you flown it before?"

"This is my first time. I've never flown supersonic before!"

"It's an amazing plane. Newly designed to eliminate the window-cracking sonic booms that haunted the original Concorde and limited its supersonic flight to overwater operations."

Usually, Gina was annoyed with cab drivers that chatted the entire trip, but the man seemed to have a lot of interesting things to say.

"Why did the Concorde create those sonic booms?" she asked.

Looking up at her in the rearview mirror, the cab driver smiled, happy to have a passenger interested in airplanes.

"Well, an airplane flows through the air like a boat flows through the water. When the water flows around the hull of the boat, it makes waves that flow outward and create a bubbling wake."

Gina pictured the Navy ships her father had served on.

"So, does an airplane create waves of air that flow outward too?" she asked.

"Yeah, exactly," the cab driver said, impressed with her intuition. "As the plane approaches the speed of sound, the waves compress in front of it. At sea level, that speed is 750 miles per hour or, roughly, 1130 kilometers per hour."

"But it changes with the airplane's altitude?" Gina asked.

"Yes!" responded the man. *She's asking the right questions.* "The speed of sound depends on many things, but air temperature has a big role. At higher altitudes, the temperature is lower, making the speed of sound slower."

"If a plane is able to fly at really high altitudes, is it easier for it to break the sound barrier?"

"Exactly. That's why the Concorde II flies at about 60,000 feet above sea level, while regular commercial jets only fly at about 30,000 feet."

"And I thought my office was high up there," Gina added playfully.

"Where were we? Oh, right. Those waves in the air compact at the nose of the plane and form a wall, known as the sound barrier. Now, standard commercial flights can't break through this barrier. They travel at speeds lower than the speed of sound. In other words, they are subsonic. But the design of the Concorde and other supersonic jets allows them to 'break' through the barrier. When they do this, the compressed waves at the front of the plane are released and produce an explosive boom!"

The cab driver shouted the last word and realized that, in his excitement, the taxi had begun its own acceleration towards the sound barrier. He quickly eased up on the accelerator and noticed Gina relax her grip on the passenger grab handle. "Well," he grinned, "at least we won't be late."

Gina smiled. "How do you know so much about airplanes?"

"I was in the Gulf War. Flew an F-4 Phantom. It could fly over twice the speed of sound."

They pulled up to the terminal.

℘꧁

Inside the terminal, she was guided to a private waiting room that oozed luxury. Coffee dispensers, serving fresh cups of richly-flavored coffee, and single-serving ovens baking fresh chocolate croissants at the push of a button, were arranged between cushioned chairs and small tables with reading lamps. In front of the waiting room was a wide, light-regulated window that blocked direct sunlight, but which gave a clear view of the airport and, in particular, the waiting Concorde II.

The plane was pure white with triangular, sweptback wings, its needle-point nose cocked down to allow for normal flight speeds during takeoff and landing. Once airborne, the nose would rise up to a complete needle-point position for speeds greater than twice the speed of sound, or Mach 2+.

Inside the airplane were two wide, reclining seats on each side of the aisle. When the passengers were seated and the main cabin doors closed, the captain welcomed the passengers. After describing the safety basics, she said, "For our first time passengers, we welcome you. We hope that after you have enjoyed supersonic travel with us, you will never want to go back to the time-consuming travel of the last century. So, sit back, relax, and enjoy your unique journey on the edge of the Earth."

The captain's voice continued over the cabin speakers as she continued her welcoming remarks.

"After takeoff we will climb to our cruising altitude of 60,000 feet, twice as high as ordinary jet aircraft, where the ride will be quiet and smooth regardless of the storms below. The weather at our destination is 70° F (21.1° C) and the sky is cloudless. Our craft crew will come around soon to serve you refreshments during our short flight.

"Your personal flight screen will display our speed. Mach 1 is the speed of sound. You will be travelling at roughly Mach 2.

174

You will be pleasantly surprised that, because of the design of this craft, you will not even feel us passing through what used to be the feared 'sound barrier.'

"Also," she added, "don't worry if you momentarily feel a little heavy from the pull against gravity as our powerful engines lift us quickly to our altitude."

Gina didn't fully understand what she meant until after the plane lifted smoothly from the runway and circled gently out over the Atlantic Ocean.

Once over the water, the airplane kicked in its afterburners. In an instant she felt a thrust upward as the plane maneuvered into a steep climb, she felt as if an invisible force was sucking the airplane upward in an elevator ride faster than she had ever experienced, while pressing her gently into her seat.

Within a few minutes, the airplane leveled, and they were in the upper stratosphere.

Below, the ground disappeared into a haze of clouds. She looked out and was surprised to see that even though it was daytime, the sky was a dark, indigo blue. The curvature of the Earth was rimmed with a ribbon of white and blue. She watched in fascination until she became accustomed to the view. When she settled back, she began to consider why she was on the flight.

Her computer check of the Institute and Li Chow had not been helpful. Li Chow was connected to a large company, *Artefice Instituto*, as a vice president and board member. Xylem Robotic Institute didn't come up at all when she searched it.

She didn't pursue the search further, figuring the mystery would soon be revealed anyway. She sat back, relaxed and decided to let the adventure unfold. Surely there was an interesting reason for the strange invitation.

As she gazed out the oval window, sipping an aromatic cup of espresso, she realized that in the frenzy of her life, she rarely took the time to simply sit back and let her thoughts wander. For a few minutes, she let her mind take her back to her earlier years. Most of her thoughts were of college. There, she felt she had suddenly been set free to control her time and her life. What a great adventure it had been. She remembered that her studies were difficult, but young freedom was delicious and she'd thrived. Then there was the workplace. Opportunities opened for her, and now she was in New York City—the Big Apple.

She thought back to her childhood. As the child of a naval officer, she had been in many schools and many countries. There were always new classmates, except at the end of middle school and in high school where she remained in the same house while her father had a long tour of duty at the U.S. Navy Yard in Washington, D.C. and then at the Pentagon. There she had the chance to complete high school in one place. She was so glad she met her close friends, Tad and Max. And, of course, there had been Leonard, the reincarnated Leonardo da Vinci. Had it been a dream? No, of course not, because there was the boy Leonard, who throughout high school was a daily adventure all by himself—brilliant at some moments, childlike in wonder at others and, usually, in trouble. The more she remembered, the more she smiled. As the memories returned, she wondered if she should begin to write down some of the adventures with the reincarnated Leonardo da Vinci. *What a great book that would be. I should capture it before the memories fade completely from my mind.*

What about her friends, Tad and Max? She remembered that when she had told her father that her really great friends would be her friends for life, he advised her not to be surprised at how quickly high school friendships would slip away as she embraced the freedom and new friends in college, followed by yet another setting, the work place. He had been right. The comradeship she had shared with Tad, Max, and Leonard had been replaced by new friends, interests, and adventures. Still, she had continued to keep in touch with Max and Tad, but now, being together again in person would be exciting—a new adventure—whatever it was going to be.

She soon dozed off, only to be awakened by the announcement that they were over Denver and about to begin their descent into Oakland.

At the airport, she had barely stepped past the security exit when she saw Max. "Max! Max!" she screamed as she raced toward him and embraced him for a big welcome hug. "My, goodness, Max, you look important! The mustache and beard make you look like quite the professor."

"And you look fabulous, my dear Gina!" he replied, filling his face with a broad smile as he grabbed her carry-on bag and guided her toward the exit. It was a quick ride to Jack London Square and the Waterfront Hotel, a comfortable, three story, boutique hotel.

"I love the commanding flecks of grey," Gina retorted. "The pixels don't do you justice. How are you? It's great to see you in the flesh!"

As they entered, Gina looked around the lobby. In a far corner, a man stood gazing out of the window at the activity along the waterfront outside of the hotel. He had his back to her. Tall, with broad shoulders and short, military-cropped hair, he was trimly dressed in slacks and a casual sweater. It had to be Tad. She tapped Max and pointed to the tall stranger. "What? Oh, yes," said Max. "Hey, stranger," yelled Max, "you hiding in the corner or do you want to come say hello to your oldest friends?"

Hearing a familiar voice, Tad spun around and caught his breath as he recognized Gina and Max.

"Hey!" he exclaimed happily. "You are both a sight for sore eyes. Max, you're amazingly distinguished, as usual. And Gina, you're a welcome and beautiful vision!"

They rushed together and wrapped in a three-way hug. At last Gina said, "I'm so excited that we're together again, even if it's because our Leonard is in trouble, as Max suggests."

Tad, his face matured by his military experience, beamed his own delight. "Yeah, me too. This is awesome."

He paused and then said, "But what do you think, Max? Why do you think we're here?"

"It's obvious. We're the only people who know who he really is, and somehow, I'm guessing that there is no one else he could turn to without having to explain his reincarnation."

"I don't know," said Tad. "He disappeared from our lives a long time ago. After all, it's been almost two decades since we last heard from him."

"But Tad," reminded Gina, "you remember that Leonard and his troubles were our burden and our fun back in high school."

"And the clue," said Max, "is in the name, Xylem. But why guess? The way to solve the mystery is by following the directions and going there."

He retrieved a waiting envelope from the hotel registration desk. Opening it, he read, "Follow this map to the corner of Clay and 4th Street. Enter at the Clay Street entrance."

"Lead on," said Tad.

"I'm right behind you," said Gina, almost ready to skip in schoolgirl fashion.

Holding the map, Max led Gina and Tad down Embarcadero, across the streetcar tracks and along Clay to 4th Street. The building at the corner was stark. The windows were dark, and the plainness of the building seemed to portend a disappointing ending to the mysterious notes.

Tad took the large door handle, twisted it and cautiously pulled open the front door. They carefully stepped in. Once inside, they were pleasantly surprised. The building seemed larger than its exterior had suggested. The reception area was bright, with rich reds and soft rose colors. A receptionist greeted them. "Hello, Ms. Brunelli, Dr. Peabody, and Mr. Sullivan. We've been expecting you. Please, follow me." They passed down a long hallway. The building smelled of acetate and orange peels mixed with a suggestion of another odor they could not identify. The trace odor was faintly unpleasant.

They were led into a softly-lit waiting room filled with modern furniture. *Old Ikea*, Gina mused. In a far corner, a tall man with black hair pulled tightly back into a ponytail rose to greet them.

"Good afternoon," he said, "I am Dr. Li Chow. I welcome you to our humble work place. The boss has been anxiously awaiting your arrival. Please do accompany me."

He turned toward an open hallway as he beckoned them to follow.

The hallway ended at a massive white wall. They were surprised when Dr. Chow began speaking to it.

"We are all here," he announced.

The wall in front of them groaned, hummed, and then, slowly, the entire wall opened, revealing a laboratory filled with long, stainless steel machines, blinking lights, and eerie sounds they could not identify. Standing in the middle, surrounded by a number of men and women all wearing white lab coats, stood none other than Leonard Vinciti, looking surprisingly like the Leonardo da Vinci they first encountered in Florence, but without the beard or the long hair. He hurried to greet them, shaking hands with Tad and Max and giving Gina a big bear hug. "It's been a long time," he said. "I just had to find you three."

"You must be in big trouble to get us all here after all these years?" inquired Max.

"I'm glad you remembered that we have always been on your side," said Gina, reassuringly.

"Not to mention that you always had the craziest problems," added Tad.

"Oh, did you guys think I brought you here because I was in trouble?" asked Leonard. Then he laughed a hardy laugh. Shaking his head, he said, "That's rich. Typical of your kindness, your loyalty, and belief in my do-over. But no, my dear friends. This is most decidedly not bad news. It is good news that I now want to share."

"No," said Leonard, waving his arms expansively, "make that *great* news."

"What is it?" asked Tad.

"Tell us!" demanded Gina.

"I needed to get you all here before it is announced to the world."

"Does this have to do with the name of your company," asked Max. " Does it have a meaning?"

"Yes. Plants." His broad grin telegraphed his enjoyment of this meeting.

Gina examined their host. *I shouldn't be surprised that the teenage Leonard Vinciti has matured, looking much more like the man we met so many years ago in Florence. I wonder if anyone else notices how much he looks like Leonardo da Vinci. Then again, even though there were sketches preserved from the Renaissance, there were no photographs or videos except the ones in the cameras of those Japanese tourists or perhaps from tourists during the spectacle in the piazza. Also, he had no beard.*

The laboratory walls were pure white plaster, painted with an eclectic selection of character sketches, along with patches of beautifully painted scenes of the Rocky Mountains, the palisades of the Pacific Ocean and, in between, scenes from Tuscany. Also on the wall were ReadyBoards where Xylem employees were writing complex mathematical equations while the ReadyBoards automatically calculated and printed the answers. They all stood back and watched. Chemical formulas and diagrams of molecular structures with double helixes were strangely appearing, seemingly unaided. Occasionally a horse's head would appear for no apparent reason.

Leonard swept his hand around to display his laboratory. "I took a lesson from your famous inventor, Thomas Edison. He had so many new ideas that he needed a staff to devote their time to his experiments. I read that when he conceived of the idea of a flameless light from electrical resistance, he hired assistants to test and try hundreds of different materials until they found the right material for the filament that eventually became the core of the electric light bulb. Then he had even more people help him to commercialize and sell it. "I have done the same with my work. Soon I'll need more staff to market and sell my new product."

"A new product?" asked Gina.

"Yes, and I want you all to be part of this new future."

"What is that?" asked Max.

"My dear friends, I have found the answer to my quest to invent or discover something for the betterment of mankind—make that *human*kind."

He paused, looked carefully at each of them, then continued proudly, "I have attained my goal."

"Is that what all these people have been working on for you?" Tad asked.

"No, not *for* me, *with* me. A team working together like in my youth in the studio of Andrea del Verrocchio," said Leonard.

"Doing what?" asked Tad.

"Testing thousands of plants and trees."

Gina gave him a puzzled look. "Plants? What for?"

"I'll show you in just a minute. First, look at this. Sometimes I invent things just for fun." He led them to a small alcove with a window that overlooked a vacant lot.

Dr. Chow passed Leonard a tablet. Gina, Tad, and Max watched as Leonard's hands navigated through numerous apps and documents. He finally clicked on an icon of an old typewriter.

"Here, Gina, type anything you want," Leonard grinned as he passed the tablet to her.

She sat down and began to type:

All good things come to those who wait

The display read:

Tutte le cose buone arrivano per chi sa aspettare

except the characters were written backwards:

Tutte le cose buone arrivano per chi sa aspettare

They all laughed in surprise.

Gina was intrigued. "The famous Leonardo mirror-writing goes hi-tech!"

"This is where I record my daily notes," he said. "But enough of this. Come, follow me." As he spoke, he went to a nearby cabinet, opened the doors and removed a packet of invoices. He handed the packet to them to examine. "Take a look at these," he said proudly.

"Sure," said Max, thumbing through the packet. "These are electricity invoices from Pacific Gas & Electric. What do they mean?"

181

"Examine them closely," instructed Leonard.

"Look," said Gina, "there are no charges, only credits. Leonard, you've been selling electricity to the power company." She studied the package. "And you're increasing your sales every month."

"Exactly," boasted Leonard.

"Solar panels on the roof?" asked Tad.

"Wind turbines in the parking lot?" guessed Gina.

"Geothermal in the basement?" speculated Max.

"No," replied Leonardo, a huge grin on his face. "Follow me."

He led them to an outside door. He paused to look into an eye scanner. The heavy door swung open. Inside was a vast, walled courtyard filled with an odd assortment of plants and trees growing in neat rows. At the end of one row was a large, misshapen tree. As they stepped through the door into the courtyard, they were overwhelmed by a terrible odor.

It seemed to be a witch's mixture of vomit and rotten eggs.

"Yuck!" said Gina, gagging. "What is that gross smell? Are you generating sulfur?"

Tad and Max put their hands over their noses.

Leonard nodded. "That is a Ginkgo Biloba tree. Unfortunately, I made a mistake and grew a female tree instead of a male tree. It's only the fruit of the female Ginkgo tree that stinks. It took me years to grow this tree, so I have to wait for my new crop, which will be all male. Until I can grow some males, I'm stuck with stink. But no matter, you get used to it."

"What's a Ginkgo tree?" Gina was holding her nose.

"Why a Ginkgo Biloba?" asked Max. "I know that a Ginkgo tree is a holdover survivor from prehistoric times like ants, sharks, and alligators, but why the Ginkgo?"

"I don't know exactly," replied Leonard, "but it works. There's something about the ancient wood structure. That's the magic—this sole surviving tree from prehistoric times is now the ticket for unlimited energy from the sun. It will be the future of the world. It is going to be my salvation and perhaps a future fortune for me and for all of you, too."

"What does it do?" asked Tad.

"Why, it produces electricity directly from the sun."

"How does it do that?" Tad looked confused.

"After many years of experimenting, I refined magnetic iron atoms and created a nano-electrical-mechanical system that I designed to work with nano-robotic manipulations. It merges at the atomic level into the DNA of the molecules in the chloroplasts of the leaves of the Ginkgo tree. The light energy from the sun—through photosynthesis—is intensified by the molecular robot armed with magnetic iron atoms to produce a powerful electric current. I tried thousands of plants, but my idea would not work until I finally tried it with the Ginkgo. The moment I inserted and integrated my adapted atoms and robotic molecules into the tree trunk, I received a powerful, jolting electric shock. I cried out in pain and joy at the same time."

"The tree is actually directly generating electricity?" asked Tad.

"Indeed it does," said Leonard. "It's a grand old tree, can live for hundreds of years in the worst climate and soil conditions. It's a tough tree. That's why it has survived since prehistoric times. One Ginkgo tree even survived the atomic bomb blast on Hiroshima during World War II. This tree not only provides all the electricity I need for my laboratory, but I'm making money selling electricity back to the power company. The joy of it all is that this is only the beginning. Soon, other modified Ginkgo trees will become the power plants of the future, a future that has arrived.

"This is, my dear friends, who never doubted me, the moment at the end of my quest—my El Dorado. Happily, I will now be allowed to live out my new life in this wonderful country and in this wonderful century."

Tad looked around in amazement. "Leonard, are you saying that you can produce enough electricity for the whole world?"

"Not just me," said Leonard, "but it will be available for the entire world." He continued, "Picture beautiful forests of trees, giant forests, perhaps, in national parks, with thousands, maybe millions of trees, each tree modified and wired to provide the electric power needed for an entire nation. An endless source of clean power from a beautiful forest of trees. That, my friends, is the artificial photosynthesis you advised me to pursue."

"It was Max," said Gina, looking at the math professor on the other side of Tad.

"I haven't forgotten, and I am forever grateful," replied Leonard, nodding toward Max, who acknowledged the nod with a nod of his own. Max loved being right. "Here, take a look," said Leonard as he opened a large box next to the tree. The bottom of the box was glass, which allowed the viewer to look down and see the root system. Wires from inside the tree were linked to a series of electrical connections from which other wires snaked away and disappeared underground. "The sunlight-absorbing leaves now provide a direct conversion of solar energy to usable electric power." Leonard was beaming.

The three friends quietly applauded, their faces filled with pride.

"But that's not the best part," Leonard added excitedly.

"I kind of thought it was," quipped Gina, grinning.

"No, the best part is that the City Council of Florence, in partnership with the Italian National Academy of Science, created the Leonardo da Vinci Award in Science to honor me posthumously as the hero of 16th century Florence and the Father of the Renaissance. The award is given once every five years for the greatest advancement in the development of energy sources by an Italian or anyone of Italian descent. This is the highest award in science awarded by the Italian government and it is a highly prestigious award that has recently gained recognition throughout the world. Next year will be only the second time the award will have been given. Also, next year the award will be given in the auditorium at the *Università Degli Studi* in Florence."

Gina, Tad and Max each looked at each other. Leonard shrugged, smirking. "I know it's egotistical, but I have always been sure of myself. When I make the announcement of this invention at the Energy Producers Convention in New York next week, I am optimistically confident that Xylem Robotics and its founder, Leonard Vinciti, will be the recipient of this prestigious award. After all, my invention means clean, cheap, electrical energy for the world. When that happens, you three will be there and Max will be on the podium next to me to be acknowledged for his brilliance in introducing me to the concept that is now this reality.

"And," he added, "if anyone recognizes me, Leonard Vinciti, the Leonardo da Vinci look-alike, receiving the Leonardo da Vinci Award, then it will be even more fun."

Leonard noticed that, as he spoke, his three friends were beaming approval. Gina reached over and clasped Tad's shoulder while Tad placed an arm around her waist and his other hand on Max's shoulder. They were together again.

Then Leonard grinned mischievously, looked at each of them, and added, "Maybe I'll even sing a song."

Who was the Real Leonardo da Vinci?

Leonardo da Vinci was born in a farm house near the town of Vinci, Italy on Saturday, April 15, 1452. He was the illegitimate son of Ser Piero da Vinci and a local maiden, Chaterina. As a baby, he was taken into his father's household and raised by his father and his stepmother, Albiera.

His early childhood was mostly spent roaming the local countryside with his Uncle Francesco. When he became a teenager, Leonardo's father moved the family from Vinci to Florence, in the hope that his son would follow in his footsteps and become a notary. It was in Florence that da Vinci began his education, but it became obvious that he was more interested in art than matters of law. Recognizing his son's talent, his father apprenticed Leonardo to the art studio of Andrea Verrocchio. Here, Leonardo honed his skills in painting and sculpting and, later, opened his own studio, soon establishing himself as Florence's leading artist.

Leonardo da Vinci's interests and achievements expanded beyond his artistic talents. He was self-educated and became famous in the fields of architecture, physics, astronomy, botany, geology, anatomy, hydraulics, machinery, and military weaponry. His notations, drawings, and essays on these filled thousands of pages in notebooks—now referred to as codices. They included his ideas for hundreds of inventions, such as flying machines, a parachute, a submarine, a diving suit, an automobile, a bicycle, and various military weapons. Although lost for centuries, many were found and, today, roughly four thousand pages are preserved in various places around the world.

As illustrated by his detailed codices, da Vinci was a firm believer in discovery by close observation. His adherence to this method led him to perform over 30 human dissections and diagram the human anatomy in detail. Many of these medical drawings are still highly regarded today. Rejecting the then accepted practice of reaching medical and scientific conclusions by scholarly discussion, he is considered by many to be the father of the modern scientific process.

As skilled with his hands as his mind, Leonardo was ambidextrous and painted with either hand and, sometimes, with both. He mimicked the practices of Hebrew and Arabic writing and easily wrote from right to left instead of left to right. Thus, da Vinci developed his famous mirror writing, which can only be read by looking at the text in a mirror.

He is perhaps best known as the artist who painted the *Mona Lisa* and *The Last Supper*, but is also widely recognized by scholars as the genius of the Renaissance.

For most of his adult life, he lived either in Florence or Milan, although he did spend some time in Rome and, later, in Venice. When he was 67, the King of France, Francis I, invited him to settle in a palatial villa near Tours, France, so the king could enjoy his company and benefit from his wisdom. It was there, on May 2, 1519, that Leonardo da Vinci passed away.

$$F_n = F_{n-1} + F$$
$$0, F_1 = 1$$

Continue Reading about Leonardo da Vinci (and other subjects)

Discovering the Life of Leonardo da Vinci by Serge Bramly, translated by Sian Reynolds, HarperCollins, NY, 1991.

How to Think Like Leonardo da Vinci by Michael J. Gelb, Dell Publishing, NY, 2000.

Leonardo: Art and Science by Claudio Pescio, Guinti Gruppo Editoriale, Firenze, Italy, 2000.

Leonardo da Vinci by Kathleen Kruli, illustrated by Boris Kulikov, Puffin Books, NY, 2008.

Leonardo da Vinci by Sherwin B. Nuland, A Lipper/Viking Book, NY, 2000.

Leonardo da Vinci: Dreams, Schemes & Flying Machines by Heinz Kuhne, Prestel Publishers Ltd., Munich, Germany, 1999.

Leonardo da Vinci: The Mind of the Renaissance by Alessandro Vezzosi, Harry N. Abrams, Inc., NY, 1997.

Leonardo: Portrait of a Master by Bruno Nardini, translated by Catherine Frost, Giunti Gruppo Editoriale, Firenze, Italy, 1999.

Leonardo: The First Scientist by Michael White, St. Martin's Griffin, NY, 2000.

Leonardo: The Machines by Carlo Pedretti, translated by Catherine Frost, Giunti Gruppo Editoriale, Firenze, Italy, 1999.

Leonardo's Legacy: How Da Vinci Reimagined the World by Stefan Klein, translated by Shelley Frisch, Da Capo Press, MA, 2010.

Leonardo's Notebooks edited by H. Anna Suh, Black Dog and Leventhal Publishers, Inc., NY, 2005.

The Science of Leonardo by Fritjof Capra, Anchor Books, NY, 2007.

Who Was Leonardo da Vinci by Roberta Edwards, illustrated by True Kelley, Grosset & Dunlop, NY, 2005.

Other Subjects

Airplane Flying Handbook, FAA Handbooks, Federal Aviation Administration, DC, 2004.

Atoms: Chemicals in Action by Chris Oxlade, Heinemann Library, IL, 2007.

Basic Electricity by Nooger Van Valkenburgh, Cengage Learning, CT, 1992.

Bicycle History: A chronicle of Cycling, History of People, Races and Technology by James L. Withererell, McGann Publishing LLC., AR, 2010.

Bicycle: The History by David V. Herlihy, Quebecor World, MA, 2004.

Blockhead: The Life of Fibonacci by Joseph D'Agnese and Jolia O'Brien, Henry Holt and Company, NY, 2010.

Earth's Outer Atmosphere: Bordering Space (Earth's Sphere) by Gregory Vogt, Twenty-First Century Books, MN, 2007.

Electricity by Steve Parker, DK Eyewitness Books, England, 2005.

Gases, Pressure and Wind: The Science of the Atmosphere (Weatherwise) by Paul Fleisher, Lerner Publishing Company, MN, 2010.

Ginkgo: The Tree that Time Forgot by Peter Crane, Yale University Press, New Haven, CT, 2013.

Outbreak: Disease Detectives at Work, by Mark P. Friedlander, Jr., Twenty-First Century Books, MN, 2009.

Pilot's Handbook of Aeronautical Knowledge, FAA Handbooks, Federal Aviation Administration, DC, 2008.

Stick and Rudder: An Explanation of the Art of Flying by Wolfgang Langeweisch, McGraw Hill Professional, NY, 1990.

The (Fabulous) Fibonacci Numbers by Alfred S. Posamentoer and Igmar Lehmann, Prometheus Books, NY, 2007.

The Golden Ratio: The Story of PHI, The World's Most Astonishing Number by Mario Livio, Broadway Books, NY, 2002.

The Immune System: Your Body's Disease Fighting Army by Mark P. Friedlander, Jr. and Terry M. Phillips, Lerner Publishing Co., MN, 1998.

The Naming of America by John Hessler, The Library of Congress, D.C., 2008.

Glossary

Aileron
A movable airfoil at the trailing edge of an airplane wing that is used to initiate a rolling motion, especially in banking for turns.

Altimeter
An instrument inside an airplane's cockpit that reports how high the airplane is above sea level.

Altitude
The height of anything above a given planetary reference plane, usually the level of the sea on earth.

Amerigo Vespucci
An Italian navigator and map-maker whose name was placed on a map of the new world by Martin Waldseemuller as the origin of the name, America.

Antibiotic
An agent designed to kill or inhibit the growth of harmful bacteria.

Atom
The basic unit of matter consisting of a dense central nucleus surrounded by a cloud of negatively-charged electrons.

Bacteria
Microscopic organisms involved in fermentation, putrefaction, infectious diseases, and nitrogen fixation.

Battle of Anghiari
A battle between the armies of Milan and Florence on the plains of Anghiari, on June 29, 1440. In 1542, Leonardo da Vinci was employed to paint a giant fresco depicting the battle. He started to paint it, but did not finish. Investigators are currently determining if Leonardo da Vinci's fresco still exists behind the new wall.

Battle of Cascina
A battle between the armies of Florence and Pisa near the town of Cascina on July 28, 1364. In 1542, Michelangelo Buonarroti was employed to paint a giant fresco across from Leonardo da Vinci's fresco. Michelangelo made sketches, but did not finish the painting because the Pope summoned him to Rome.

Bernoulli's Principle
The principle that states that pressure in a stream of fluid (gas or liquid) decreases as the speed of the stream increases.

Black Death
A form of the bubonic plague that spread across Europe in the 14th century. It is estimated to have killed 30–60% of Europe's total population.

Blood Cells
Any of the cellular elements of blood, including white and red blood cells. Red blood cells primarily carry oxygen and collect carbon dioxide. White blood cells defend the body against both infectious diseases and foreign materials. See Cell.

Bloodletting
The ancient practice of withdrawing blood from a patient to cure or prevent illness and disease. See Humors.

Cell
The smallest working unit of a living thing, usually microscopic and made up of cytoplasm and a nucleus inside of a membrane.

Chinotto
A carbonated soft drink popular in Italy. It is made from oranges grown on a myrtle-leaved orange tree.

Circumference
The measurement of the distance around a circle. The term describes the outline of a circle. The circumference of a circle is found by multiplying the length of the diameter by pi. See Diameter, Pi.

Codex
An ancient manuscript. Leonardo da Vinci filled many codices with notes and sketches describing his thoughts and insights. Over 4,000 pages have been discovered.

Commission
A specific task for which someone will be paid.

Crimean Peninsula
The geographic area known as Crimea, a peninsula that is part of Ukraine. This peninsula juts into the Black Sea. Its ports were important trade routes between East Asia and Europe.

Diameter
A straight line from one point on a circle, through the center, to the opposite side; also, the length of that line.
See Circumference, Pi.

Don Quixote

The fictional "mad knight" of the famous and classic 17th century novel of a play within a play written by Spanish novelist, Miguel de Cervantes. This novel was the basis for the award winning play, and, later the musical, *Man of La Mancha.*

Drag

The force causing an object to resist movement. An aircraft in flight produces aerodynamic drag from friction as it moves through the air and from pressure distributions over the aircraft surface.

Ebbing

Moving away from land; also, gradually lessening or reducing.

Fibonacci Sequence

The infinite sequence of numbers in which each member is the sum of the previous two.

Fleur-de-lis

A symbol using three petals of a lily flower as a design, often found on a badge or coin. It was adopted as a symbol of the city of Florence and can be seen on their old currency.

Florin

A form of gold coin or money used in Florence from the 1200s to the 1500s.

Fresco

The art of painting on a moist plaster wall. A famous example is Leonardo da Vinci's *The Last Supper.*

Friction

The force that opposes motion.

Golden Rectangle

A rectangle whose side lengths are in the "Golden Ratio" of 1.618. It can be cut into a square and another rectangle with the same dimensions as itself.

Golden Spiral

A graphic representation of the Fibonacci Sequence. See Fibonacci Sequence.

Gravity

The force of attraction between all matter. The force of gravity is determined by the mass of the matter and the distance between masses (Newton's Universal Law of Gravity). The greater the mass, the shorter the distance, the greater the force.

Gregorian chant

An ancient ritual song performed in the Roman Catholic Church, usually performed by more than one person.

Humors; Humoralism

An ancient clinical belief that the body is composed of four humors (blood, phlegm, yellow bile, and black bile), and that one's health depends on their balance. Bloodletting was practiced to adjust one of the four humors in an attempt to heal patients. See Bloodletting.

Hypotenuse

The longest side of a right-angled triangle; the side opposite the right angle.

Lira

The former currency of Italy. Its use was discontinued in 2002 when Italy adopted the Euro as its new currency. Plural is Lire.

Mach

The ratio of the speed of something to the speed of sound in the medium through which the object is moving. Often used with a numeral (such as Mach 1, Mach 2, etc.) to indicate the number of times something is traveling faster than the speed of sound, for example, Mach 5 is five times faster than the speed of sound.

Mags; Magneto

A small electric generator with an armature that rotates in a magnetic field provided by permanent magnets. It supplies ignition current for certain types of internal combustion engines. In airplanes, it refers to the separate ignition system.

Mercenary

A person hired and paid to fight as a soldier in the service of a country not his/her own.

Microbe

A microorganism such as bacteria, yeast, or protozoa.

Microscope

An optical instrument with a magnifying glass, or combination of lenses, for inspecting objects too small to see with an unaided eye.

Mire

A situation or state of difficulty, distress, or embarrassment from which it is hard to extricate oneself.

Numismatic

Pertaining to, or consisting of coins, medals, paper money, or other currency.

Nung Shu

A Chinese encyclopedia given by Chinese envoys when they visited Italy, and particularly Florence, in the 15th century.

Parthenon

A Greek temple built during the 5th century B.C.E. on the Acropolis, a hill overlooking the city of Athens, and dedicated to the Greek goddess, Athena.

Phlegm

A thick mucus that develops naturally in the airways of the human body. As used in this book, the word relates to the understanding of disease in the time of Leonardo da Vinci. Phlegm was one of the four humors. See Humors.

Photosynthesis

A process used by plants and other organisms that, with chlorophyll, uses light energy, carbon dioxide, and water to manufacture food in the form of simple sugars.

Pi

A number, estimated at 3.14, referring to the number of times the length of the diameter of a circle would need to be repeated to equal the length of the circumference. See Diameter, Circumference.

Plague, Black

See Black Death.

Prism

A transparent optical element with flat, polished surfaces that refract light, so that white light is separated into the colors of the rainbow.

Protozoa

A single-celled animal.

Plethora

An amount greater than what is needed.

Pneumatic

Filled with air. When referencing tires, pneumatic means a tire filled with air instead of a solid rubber tire.

Recursive sequence
The process of choosing a starting term and repeatedly applying the same process to each term to arrive at the following term. A Fibonacci number is determined this way.

Reenactor
Someone who enacts a role from an event that occurred in history.

Renaissance
A cultural movement that spanned Europe from the 14th to the 17th centuries involving a great period of revival of art and learning. The Renaissance began in Florence, Italy, in the late Middle Ages before slowly spreading to the rest of Italy and Europe. The term comes from the Latin *renascere*, which means "rebirth." Leonardo da Vinci is widely considered the genius of the Renaissance.

Rudder
A directional control surface attached to the airplane tail (vertical stabilizer) that allows the pilot to control yaw about the vertical axis. The rudder, in conjunction with the ailerons, allows the pilot to steer the aircraft and make horizontal course changes.

Salves
An ointment applied to the skin to help heal or provide protection.

Soldo
A silver coin of lesser value than a gold florin. In the 15th century in Florence, a gold florin was worth 90 soldi. Plural is soldi.

Sonic Boom
The sound associated with shock waves created by an object traveling through air faster than the speed of sound. It transforms enormous amounts of energy into the sound of an explosion.

Sound barrier
The point at which an object moves from subsonic to supersonic speed.

Sprocket
A disc with teeth around the edge to catch and hold a moving chain.

Stratosphere
The second major layer of Earth's atmosphere, just above the troposphere and below the mesosphere. At moderate latitudes, the stratosphere is situated between approximately 6–8 miles (10–13 km) and 31 miles (50 km) above the earth's surface.

Supersonic
   Any speed above the speed of sound. The speed of sound varies
   with temperature and altitude. At sea level, in dry air at 68°F
   (20°C), the speed of sound is 767 miles per hour (1,234
   kilometers per hour). See Sonic Boom, Sound Barrier, Mach.

Thrust
   A pushing force.

Torque
   A force that rotates or turns things about an axis.

Virus
   A small infectious agent, generally made up of a nucleic acid
   molecule, that can only reproduce inside the living cells of other
   organisms.

Vlax Romani
   The most widely-spoken dialect subgroup of the Romani
   language worldwide. It is spoken mainly in Southeastern
   Europe by Romani people.

Yoke
   A device used for piloting some fixed-wing aircraft, the 'steering
   wheel' of a plane.

Yersinia Pestis
   The bacteria that carried the bubonic plague.

Zuccotto
   A Florentine frozen dessert made with ice cream, cake, and
   brandy, shaped liked the top half of a pumpkin.

Index

A

B

C

D

E

F

G

H

L

M

Mach, 174, 196
Mags (Magneto), 92, 196
Mercenary, 115, 196
Microbe, 76-80, 196
Microscope, 76-77, 110, 147-150, 166, 196
Mona Lisa Gherardini; la Gioconda, 19, 56, 58-59, 128-132, 134, 136, 188

N

Nazione, La, 83, 98-100
Nano, 183
Numismatic, 67, 197
Nung Shu, 144-146, 197

P

Parthenon, 132, 197
Penicillin, 77
Photosynthesis, 143-145, 149, 150, 152, 167, 168, 173, 185, 186, 197
Pi, 51, 194, 197
Plague, Black, 71, 77
Pressure, 92, 95
Prism, 19, 167, 197
Propeller, 91, 93, 100
Protozoa, 76-78, 196-197

R

Rabbits, 135
Rats, 74
Recursive sequence, 136, 198
Reenactor, 1, 30-36, 41, 44, 46, 96, 162, 198
Reincarnation, 64-65, 107, 142, 151, 158, 161-162, 176-177
Renaissance, 1, 15, 21-22, 29, 31-32, 36, 56-57, 59, 63-64, 68, 107, 117, 119, 140-141, 151, 158, 162, 180, 180, 184, 188, 198
Resistance, 91, 182
Rudder, 89-90, 93-96, 198

About the Author

Mark P. Friedlander, Jr. was born in Washington, D.C. and raised on the farms of Fairfax County, Virginia. He attended and graduated from the University of Virginia with a major in procrastination and served in the Air Force as an aviator during the Korean War.

After the war, he earned a law degree from the University of Virginia and then launched a career as a trial lawyer.

He has authored and coauthored books on subjects including Shakespeare, aviation history, immunology, contagious diseases, forensic science, humor, and now Leonardo da Vinci. His passion for learning about new subjects and passing this excitement on to kids helps keep him young at heart. He can be reached at Mark@ScienceNaturally.com

About the Illustrator

Worachet Boon Sakprayoonpong was born in Bangkok, Thailand in 1994, and then moved to the U.S. at an early age. He started drawing in high school and has designed artwork ever since. Boon is currently enrolled at George Mason University, studying graphic design. He enjoyed researching the Renaissance for this project- his first book. He can be reached at Boon@ScienceNaturally.com.

Project Team

Book Cover Design:
Andrew Bartelmes, Peekskill, NY
Zoe Bernard, Washington, DC

Line Drawings and Section Illustrations:
Worachet Boon Sakprayoonpong, Falls Church, VA

Production Editor:
Aislinn Boyter, Stafford, VA

Senior Editors:
Elizabeth Burns, Park City, UT
Megan Murray, Mitchellville, MD

Associate Editors:
Zoe Bernard, Washington, DC
Erin Friedlander, Centreville, VA
Michelle Goldchain, Woodbridge, VA
Omid Khanzadeh, Washington, DC
Heather Kitt, Jefferson, IA
Melissa McClellan, Blacksburg, VA
Michael Oshnisky, Washington, DC
Ashley Parker, Washington, DC
Carlo Péan, Memphis, TN
Benjamin Suehler, Washington, DC
Crystal Vogel, Washington, DC
Zoe Waltz, Indianapolis, IN

Italian Translator:
Alex Coletti, Silver Spring, MD

Aviation Consultant:
Brad Cunnington, Bexley, OH

Front Cover images:
da Vinci: iStockPhoto, GeorgiosKollidas
Max: iStockPhoto, CEFutcher
Gina: iStockPhoto, ktaylorg
Tad: iStockPhoto, Fly_Fast

Teacher's Guide Lead Writer:
Sue Garcia, Spicewood, TX

Teacher's Guide Associate Writers:
Melissa McClellan, Blacksburg, VA
Joan Wagner, Saratoga Springs, NY

Check Out More
Award Winning Titles
from *Science, Naturally!*

───────────○───────────

One Minute Mysteries series

65 Mysteries You Solve With Math
65 Mysteries You Solve With Science
65 MORE Mysteries You Solve With Science

───────────○───────────

101 Things… series

101 Things Everyone Should Know About Math
101 Things Everyone Should Know About Science

───────────○───────────

Blended STEM Fiction

The League of Scientists: Ghost in the Water

───────────○───────────

About *Science, Naturally!*

Science, Naturally is an independent press located in Washington, DC. We are committed to increasing science and math literacy by exploring and demystifying these topics in entertaining and enlightening ways. Our products are filled with interesting facts, important insights, and key connections across the curriculum.

We engage readers using both fiction and nonfiction strategies to make potentially intimidating subjects intriguing and accessible to scientists and mathematicians of all ages.

We are gratified by the recognition and awards we have received from the education, literacy and parenting communities. All of our books have earned the coveted "Recommends" designation from the National Science Teachers Association and our math books have been praised by the National Council of Teachers of Mathematics. Our newest science mysteries book was selected for the "Outstanding Science Trade Books for Students K-12" list. All of our books have been designated as valuable supplemental resources for schools, extended learning programs, and home education alike.

Our content aligns with the Next Generation Science Standards and supports the Common Core State Standards. Articulations to these, as well as many others, are available on our website.

All of our publications are available as E-books and foreign language editions include Spanish (and Spanish/English bilingual), Chinese, Korean, Hebrew, and Dutch—with more to come! Select titles are also available in Braille.

Science, Naturally books are distributed by National Book Network in the United States and abroad. For more information about our publications, to request a catalog, to be added to our mailing list, to explore joining our team, or to learn more about becoming a *Science, Naturally* author, please give us a call or visit us online.

We hope that you enjoy reading our books as much as we enjoy creating them!

Bridging the gap between the blackboard and the blacktop

Science, Naturally!®
725 8th Street, SE
Washington, DC 20003
202-465-4798 • Fax: 202-558-2132
Toll-free: 1-866-SCI-9876 (1-866-724-9876)
Info@ScienceNaturally.com
www.ScienceNaturally.com
/ScienceNaturally   @SciNaturally